FIFTEEN-MINUTE TALES

Eighteen stories for children

Fifteen-Minute Tales

Enid Blyton

A Dragon Book

FIFTEEN-MINUTE TALES

Copyright Enid Blyton 1936

First published by Methuen and Co. Ltd. 1936

Dragon edition published by
Mayflower Books 1971

Dragon Paperbacks are published
by Mayflower Books,
3 Upper James St., London, W.1.
Made and printed in Great Britain by
Cox & Wyman Ltd.,
London, Reading and Fakenham

Contents

FIFTEEN-MINUTE TALES

1. The Horrid Pop-out Stick

Grumps the goblin was a very horrid fellow. He had a curious stick made of ash, with a knobbly end. He used to stand this stick just inside his front gate, and then he waited for someone to go by.

As soon as anyone passed his gate the stick used to pop out and hit the pixie, brownie, or gnome until he howled for mercy. Then Grumps laughed fit to kill himself, and the tears rolled down his big nose and dripped on to the garden path. He thought it was a great joke.

The Pop-out Stick chased the passers-by down the road, thumping them all the time, and made them very angry indeed. But as Grumps's house was right in the very middle of the village, people simply had to pass it, so there was no help for it. When the goblin wanted to play his horrid joke, someone always got caught.

Nobody could stop Grumps putting his stick in the front garden whenever he thought he would. Sometimes it was there on a Saturday, and sometimes on a Monday or a Thursday. Nobody ever knew when it would come popping out and thump them.

The village folk held a meeting about it at last, to try and find out how they could stop Grumps playing his unkind trick.

'If only we could get the stick to give him as good a

9

whacking as it gives us he'd soon stop it!' said Twinkle the pixie.

'Yes, but the stick would never turn on Grumps,' said Gobbo the brownie.

'I've got an idea,' suddenly said Skippitty the gnome. 'Listen!'

He told them his plan, and they all nodded their heads, for they thought it was a good one.

'We'll do it tomorrow,' they said. 'You shall be the one to try the plan, Skippitty. If it comes off, well, you shall have ten gold pieces for yourself.'

Skippitty ran off. He went to the witch who lived on Bumble Common and asked her for a Rollaway Sixpence.

'Well, you must chop up that big pile of logs for me first,' said the witch, who never gave anything for nothing. So Skippitty set to work, and in two hours' time the witch saw that he had chopped up enough wood to last her a fortnight.

'Here is the Rollaway Sixpence that you wanted,' she said. 'It will be quite an ordinary sixpence until you whisper the word "Rollaway" under your breath.'

'Thank you,' said Skippitty, gratefully. He popped the sixpence in his pocket and went whistling home. Then he sent a note round to Grumps, asking him to come to a party the next day at four o'clock, to last till six.

The next afternoon Grumps, Gobbo, Twinkle, and many more elfin folk went to tea at Skippitty's. He gave them buns with jam on, a chocolate cake and red apples, so they were all very pleased. Then they gave Grumps the goblin a last chance to mend his ways.

'Grumps, *please* don't put your Pop-out Stick by your front gate any more,' said Skippitty.

'Ho ho!' said Grumps. 'You don't suppose I'm going to stop that, do you? No, no, it makes me laugh too much!'

The gnome said no more. It was time for his guests to go. It was night-time outside, but the moon was shining brightly. Skippitty felt in his pocket to make sure that he had the Rollaway Sixpence there.

'Good-bye, everybody,' he said. Then, just at his front gate he dropped the sixpence. It made a little tinkling noise and then lay still. Everyone looked to see it, and pretended to feel in their pockets.

'Whose is it?' asked Skippitty.

'Not mine!' said Gobbo.

'Nor mine!' said Twinkle. And everyone said the same except Grumps the goblin, who was rather greedy and not at all honest. As soon as he heard them all saying that it was not their sixpence, he pretended to feel in each of his pockets very carefully.

'Dear me, it must be mine,' he said at last. 'Yes, I had a sixpence, and it's gone. I'll pick it up.'

He stooped down to get it, and at that very moment Skippitty whispered under his breath.

'Rollaway,' he said so softly that Grumps didn't hear him.

Just as the goblin's fingers touched the magic sixpence, it stood up on its edge and rolled away. Grumps went after it. The sixpence rolled a bit farther still.

The gnomes, brownies, and pixies watched in delight.

Every time that Grumps got near to it the sixpence rolled a little farther, and soon the goblin was half-way down the street. He was quite determined to get the sixpence. All the others followed him in excitement, wondering if Skippitty's plan would work.

Grumps went on and on, and the sixpence went on too, always a little way ahead of him. He went down the hill and up again. He went along Primrose Lane, and crossed over the bridge to the High Street. The sixpence took him all round the market square, glittering in the moonlight. Grumps puffed and panted, and saw nothing but the sixpence.

Then the little magic coin ran down the road that led to Grumps's own cottage. The goblin followed, not noticing where he was going. All the others ran after him, getting more and more excited. Soon the sixpence was outside Grumps's house. It lay still on the ground, just outside his front gate.

The goblin gave a cry of triumph, and darted on it. At that very same moment it rose in the air, hit him on the nose, burst into smoke, and disappeared!

And also at that very same moment out rushed the Pop-out Stick, which Grumps had left on guard by the front gate when he had gone out to tea. It pounced on the goblin and began to whack him hard, just as it had thumped all the other villagers from time to time.

'Who's that whacking me?' cried Grumps in a rage. But just as he turned to see, the moon went behind a cloud and the street was in darkness. Grumps couldn't see what was thumping him, and he got very angry. He tried to hit back, but he only bruised his knuckles against the knobbly end of the stick.

Then he got frightened and ran away down the street. But the Pop-out Stick followed, as it had been taught to do, and had a merry time whacking him on the shoulders as he ran.

How all the pixies, gnomes, and brownies laughed to hear what was happening! It had happened to them so many times, and they were delighted that Grumps should fall into his own trap. They followed after him, keeping carefully on the other side of the road, for they didn't want to get a sudden whack from the stick too.

'Help! Mercy! Thieves! Help!' yelled Grumps. 'Skippitty, Twinkle, Gobbo! Help! Help!'

But nobody would help him – in fact, they couldn't for no one but Grumps himself knew how to stop the stick. For a long time he didn't guess what was hitting him, for he didn't know that he was near his house.

At last Skippitty thought he had had enough. So he shouted to Grumps, 'It's your own Pop-out Stick after you, Grumps. How do you like it? It's a very good joke, isn't it? We are laughing about it just as much as *you* laugh when it goes after *us*!'

Then Grumps gave a yell of surprise and anger. He shouted a magic word, and the stick rushed up the street and back into the house. Grumps went too, and the listening folk heard his door slam loudly.

'What a fine plan that was of yours!' said everyone to Skippitty. 'You have well earned the ten gold pieces. You shall have them tomorrow!'

The next day Grumps the goblin couldn't get up

because his back was hurt with all the thumping. Then the others showed what kind hearts they had, for they took him a nice jelly, swept up his house for him, and lighted his fire.

Grumps lay in bed, very much ashamed.

'Hi!' he called to Gobbo, who was lighting his fire. 'Take that old stick and break it up for firewood, will you? It will start the fire nicely.'

Then the others knew that Grumps was sorry and had learnt his lesson. Gobbo broke up the Pop-out Stick, and put it on the fire. It soon burnt up and made a curious green flame. Then it gave a sound just like a sigh, and that was the end of it!

'You forgive us, and we'll forgive *you*,' said Skippitty to Grumps. So they all forgave one another, and after that lived happily together. Skippitty got his ten gold pieces, and out of it he bought Grumps a nice new stick with a gold band round it with his name on. It was just an ordinary stick, but Grumps liked it very much indeed.

Wasn't it kind of Skippitty?

2. *The Goblin Shoes*

Once upon a time there were two children called Alice and Pip. They were very spoilt, and were not at all nice to know. Other children wouldn't play with them, so they had to play with each other, but as they quarrelled nearly all the time it wasn't much fun.

Now, one day they went for a walk into the country. They went through the woods, and were just about in the middle when Alice cried out in surprise.

'Look, Pip!' she said. 'Here's a tiny pair of shoes, standing outside this oak tree! Did you ever see such a small pair!'

Sure enough, when Pip looked he saw the tiniest red shoes he had ever seen in his life. They would not even have fitted Alice's smallest doll.

'I expect they belong to some fairy!' he said, in excitement.

'Pooh, we don't believe in fairies!' said Alice scornfully.

'Still there might be some, even if we don't believe there are,' said Pip. 'These shoes certainly couldn't belong to anyone human, could they?'

'No,' said Alice. 'Oh, Pip! *I* know! Perhaps a fairy lives in this oak tree, and has put her shoes outside to be cleaned!'

Pip knocked on the tree, and tried to find a door, but he couldn't.

'I'll tell you what we'll do,' he said. 'We'll take these home with us. Perhaps the fairy will come to fetch them, and we shall see her.'

So they picked up the tiny shoes and took them home. They placed them on a table and examined them carefully. There was no doubt at all but that the shoes must belong to one of the Little Folk, because they had certainly been worn, and one of them had a patch on at the side.

'Let's put them on the window-sill, and then if the fairy comes we shall see her,' said Alice.

'She'll probably come at night,' said Pip. 'Then we *shan't* see her, silly!'

'I'm *not* silly!' said Alice crossly. 'Can you think of anything better, then?'

Pip thought for a little while, and then he chuckled.

'I've thought of a lovely plan,' he said. 'You know that fairies can grant wishes, Alice, don't you? Well, what about catching this one and not letting her go till she has promised us three wishes?'

'Ooh, yes!' said Alice. 'But how could we catch her?'

'Let's glue the shoes tightly to the window-sill,' said Pip, 'and put glue inside the shoes too! Then when the fairy comes and slips her feet inside she won't be able to get away!'

'That's a good idea!' cried Alice. 'But won't she be cross?'

'Let her!' said Pip. '*I* shan't care, so long as I can get my three wishes!'

So the two children carried out their horrid plan. They glued the tiny shoes tightly to the wooden sill inside the window, and then poured glue inside.

No one came for them during the day, though the children kept a sharp watch. There was going to be a moon that night, so they decided to keep awake, and see if anything happened.

They drew the curtains back from the windows and the moonlight streamed inside, lighting up the little shoes very clearly. Alice and Pip lay in bed and watched them.

Suddenly they heard a tiny sound. At once they sat up in bed. Yes, someone was climbing up on to the window-ledge from the garden outside. Who could it be? If it was a fairy, surely she could fly!

A tiny figure appeared on the sill. It was an ugly little goblin! Not a fairy, after all! He was dressed in dark red, and had a pointed cap with a feather. He wore long, red stockings, but no shoes.

'Ha!' he cried, in a tiny little voice, when he saw the shoes, 'here they are!'

Then he saw the children sitting up in bed.

'You shouldn't have taken them away,' he said. 'I had left them out for the cobbler to put another patch on. The grey squirrel told me he had seen you take them, and he followed you all the way home. Then he saw them on this window-sill and ran back to tell me.'

The children said nothing. Truth to tell, they were feeling a little frightened. The goblin was so *very* ugly,

17

and he looked rather bad-tempered too. What would he say when he found he was a prisoner?

The goblin slipped his feet into the shoes, and then tried to walk away, but the glue held his feet tightly and he cried out in rage:

'You wicked children! You've played a trick on me!'

'Grant us three wishes, and we will set you free,' said Pip, in rather a quavery voice.

'What! Three wishes to horrid children like you!' cried the goblin, in a rage. 'I know all about you, nasty, horrid, quarrelsome children! Why, all the Little Folk think you are dreadful!'

Alice and Pip went very red.

'You grant us three wishes, or you'll be there till morning, and our nurse will see you,' said Pip.

The goblin scowled at them. Then a mocking smile came over his face.

'Very well,' he said. 'You shall have your three wishes. Wishes are only of use to good people, and so I am sure yours will not bring you any happiness! Now set me free.'

Pip jumped out of bed, took a sharp pen-knife, and chipped away the glue from beneath the shoes. The goblin ran off at once, and disappeared down the side of the wall into the garden. The last they heard of him was a low mocking laugh.

'Well, we've got our three wishes,' said Pip, trying to speak cheerfully.

'Oh, Pip, do you suppose that what that Goblin said is true?' said Alice. 'Do you think everyone thinks we are horrid?'

'I shouldn't wonder if they think *you* are,' said Pip. 'Girls always *are* stupid!'

'They're *not*!' said Alice, angrily. 'Boys are horrid; everyone knows that! Nurse is always saying so.'

'Be quiet!' said Pip, pulling Alice's hair very hard indeed.

'Ooh!' wept Alice, and she tried to pinch Pip. 'I wish somebody would take you right away and shake you hard!'

'And I wish the same about you!' shouted Pip.

Oh, the silly, silly children! They had quite forgotten that their wishes would come true! Hardly were the words out of their mouths than they felt themselves snatched up and whisked out of the window. For three minutes they travelled so swiftly through the air that they could hardly breathe. Then they were put down on the ground, and were shaken very hard indeed.

Alice had no breath at all, and Pip thought every hair on his head would be shaken off. For five minutes they were well shaken, and then suddenly they were set down and left alone.

They began to cry. Pip looked round and saw that they were in a small room lighted by a tiny lamp up in the ceiling. There was no furniture of any sort – not even a rug on the floor.

'Where can we be, and why did we come here?' sobbed Alice.

'We wished two stupid wishes,' groaned Pip. 'Don't you remember? Well, we must get out of here; that's certain. Wherever *can* we be?'

The two children looked carefully round the walls, but

to their alarm and astonishment they could find no door and no window. There was absolutely no way of getting out at all!

They sat down again, and looked at one another in dismay.

'Well, we'd better wait for someone to let us out,' said Alice, at last. 'What a good thing we still have one wish left. What shall we wish, Pip? Shall we wish to be very, very rich!'

'No,' said Pip. 'Let's wish to be a prince and princess.'

'Why not a king and queen?' asked Alice.

'Fancy, we could wish ourselves on the moon if we wanted to!' said Pip.

'Oh, don't do anything like that,' said Alice, beginning to cry again. 'Perhaps we're on the moon now! Oh, Pip, suppose no one comes to fetch us out! Do, do let's wish ourselves out of here back into our beds.'

'No, that would be wasting our wish,' said Pip, firmly. 'We must wait a bit. I'm sure someone will let us out.'

The children were silent for a little while, and then Alice began to talk of what the goblin had said.

'Do you think we really *are* horrid children?' she asked Pip. 'Nobody ever asks us to parties you know, and we can't get anyone to come and play with us now.'

Pip went very red. He knew quite well that they were both very horrid children indeed.

'Don't let's talk about that,' he said.

'Yes, but we must,' said Alice. 'I'd like to make friends with some girls, because I want to show them my dolls. And I'm sure you'd like to show Dick and Tom your new engine. And I *do* want to go to parties.'

'Well, perhaps we *are* rather horrid sometimes,' said Pip. 'We'll try to be nicer, shall we?'

'Could we *wish* to be nicer?' asked Alice.

'What's the good of that?' said Pip. 'We might have to stay here all the rest of our lives if we used our wish that way. I'm getting tired of being here. I vote we use our last wish in getting back home.'

'Well, listen,' said Alice. 'Let's wish that we were back home and were nicer children. Wouldn't that do?'

'That's really *two* wishes,' said Pip.

'Well, if we put the getting back home one first,' said Alice, 'we'd be safe. And there's a chance the second part of the wish might come true too. Come on, Pip, let's wish it.'

'All right,' said Pip. He stood up and spoke very loudly. 'I WISH WE WERE BOTH SAFELY BACK HOME IN OUR BEDS AND WERE NICER CHILDREN!' he said.

In a trice the tiny room vanished, something caught up the two children, and once more they were whirled through the air. Bump! They landed on something soft! When they had got back their breath they looked round. Hurrah! They were safely back in their bedroom again.

'That's good,' said Pip. 'Are you all right, Alice?'

'Yes. Are you?' asked his sister. 'What a horrid adventure, Pip! Let's go to sleep and forget all about it.'

In two minutes they were fast asleep. When they awoke the next morning they remembered all about the goblin shoes, but somehow or other they felt very much ashamed of themselves, so they said nothing about it at all.

Did the last part of their third wish come true? Well, that I don't really know; but since they have been asked to four parties already, and are giving one of their own, one of two things must have happened!

Either they have turned over a new leaf themselves, and are trying to be nice, or else the last part of the wish *did* come true. What do *you* think?

Once there was a goblin whom nobody liked. He was very mean, very selfish, and he told rather a lot of naughty stories.

His name was Feefo, and he lived in a little cottage at the end of Buttercup Village. Everyone wished he would go and live somewhere else, but he wouldn't. So they just had to put up with him.

One day he went out on to Bumble Common to pick some yellow gorse for spell-making. As he was coming home he saw a curious-looking nest in a bush. It was built of yellow gorse-blossoms, spiders' threads, and bluebells. It was the strangest nest Feefo had ever seen.

He looked into it, and saw four bright green eggs with purple spots at each end.

'Those eggs should be good for making spells!' he thought. 'I'll take them all.'

Now, of course you know that to take the eggs of birds is a most unkind thing to do. No one should take more than one, and it is better to take none at all. After all, they belong to the bird, and not to people who pass by. Feefo knew all this, but he didn't care a bit.

He looked round to see that nobody was near, for it was forbidden in Fairyland to take eggs from nests. Then he quickly took all four eggs and slipped them into his pocket.

23

Off he went home, planning how he could use the eggs for spells, for it was certain that such queer ones would be very useful. Feefo wondered what sort of a bird had laid them. He thought of all the birds he knew, but not one of them laid bright green eggs with purple spots.

Now when he got home he forgot all about the eggs in his pocket. He sat down on his stool, and crack-crack-crack! Every single one of those eggs broke!

'Ugh!' said Feefo, crossly. 'What a mess in my pocket! I must turn it inside out and go and wash it at the pump in the yard.'

So out he went, and began washing his eggy pocket under the pump. He threw the bits of broken egg-shell on the ground, and was just going indoors to dry his pocket by the fire, when he saw a very strange bird. It was bright green, and had purple spots on its head and tail.

'Boo-hoo-hoo!' it cried as it flew. 'All my eggs are gone! Who has taken them? Boo-hoo-hoo!'

As soon as Feefo saw the green bird he hurried indoors as fast as he could, for he knew it was a Cockyolly Bird, and he was afraid of what it might do to him if it found out that he had taken its eggs. But he forgot that he had left the broken egg-shells out in the yard.

The Cockyolly Bird saw them, and swooped down to them. Then it set up such a crying and howling that everyone looked out of the window to see what was the matter.

Feefo locked the door, shut all the windows and sat trembling by the fire. After a while the Cockyolly Bird stopped its crying and Feefo saw that it was gone. But he didn't open his door and windows for a very long time.

In the afternoon he thought he was safe, so he opened his door and went out to buy some butter. But whilst he was gone the Cockyolly Bird flew in and sat up in the rafters. When Feefo came back he brought a friend with him, and they both sat down to have tea.

'Feefo stole my four eggs this morning and broke them all,' suddenly said the Cockyolly Bird in a loud voice. Feefo looked up into the rafters and saw the green bird sitting there. He was frightened and angry, so he took up a cushion and threw it at the bird.

The cushion fell on to the tea-table and knocked the milk-jug over. It fell to the floor and was broken.

'He broke my eggs and now his jug is broken,' said the Cockyolly Bird, pleased.

Feefo's friend was shocked to hear that Feefo had taken all the poor bird's eggs. He said good-bye, and ran out, for he didn't like to take tea with such an unkind person. He told everyone he met about the Cockyolly Bird sitting up in the rafters, talking in a loud voice, and all the little folk were delighted to hear that the selfish goblin was being punished.

Next day lots of the village folk called to see Feefo, pretending to come and borrow this, that, and the other, but really to see if the Cockyolly Bird was still there.

The first person to knock at the door was Dinkie the elf, who asked Feefo if he could give her change for a shilling.

'You ought to tell him to change his stockings too,' said the Cockyolly Bird in a loud voice. 'He's got two tremendous big holes in each foot. I saw them when he took off his shoes last night.'

Feefo got as red as a tomato. He threw a potato at the bird, but it missed her altogether, and hit a lamp, which broke into a hundred pieces. The Cockyolly Bird laughed loudly.

The next person to call was Mother Twinkle, who asked if Feefo could let her have just a drop of milk till the milkman called.

'I haven't any,' said Feefo.

'Yes, he has!' said the Cockyolly Bird up in the rafters. 'He's got a whole jugful in the larder. I saw it there myself.'

Feefo grew very red again, and threw a slipper at the bird. But it missed once more, and broke a vase on the mantelpiece. The Cockyolly Bird laughed so much that she nearly fell off her rafter.

Mother Twinkle laughed too, and went off to tell her friends what had happened. Soon the Bee-man came to ask Feefo if he could tell him the right time.

'Quarter-past eleven,' said the goblin.

'Hi, Bee-man!' cried the Cockyolly Bird. 'I can tell you where Feefo hides all his money. It's in the china pig on the mantelpiece! You go and see!'

'Be quiet!' cried Feefo, in a rage. He flung a piece of soap at the Cockyolly Bird, and it bounced on a rafter, fell off, and hit Feefo on the head. The Cockyolly laughed till the tears streamed off its beak.

When the Bee-man had gone, Feefo looked at the bird.

'If you say another word I'll get a gun and shoot you!' he said. 'You horrid, horrid bird, go away before I do something you won't like!'

'If you go and get a gun I'll fly down and peck your nose!' cried the Cockyolly Bird, and it jumped up and down on the rafters as if it were mad.

There came another knock at the door. Feefo looked at the bird, and decided that he wouldn't open the door in case the bird said something else about him. So he crouched down behind a chair and was quite quiet.

The visitor knocked again, and still there was no answer. Then Feefo heard someone calling in at the window.

'Is there no one at home?'

He didn't answer – but the Cockyolly Bird did.

'Good morning, Your Majesty!' it cried. 'Feefo is in, and he's hiding behind the chair. He's a horrid person. He didn't wash behind his ears this morning, and he's got holes in both his stockings, and he hides his money in the china pig and pretends he hasn't any, and he tells stories, and he's taken my four eggs and broken them all!'

Feefo peeped out to see who his visitor was, and, oh, my! it was the Queen herself who had heard about the poor Cockyolly Bird's stolen eggs, and had come to ask why Feefo had taken them. The little goblin crept out from behind the chair and opened the door for the Queen to come in.

'I am very displeased with you, Feefo,' she said. 'I see that the Cockyolly Bird is punishing you, so I shall leave her to it. She shall stay here with you until you have really turned over a new leaf.'

What a dreadful punishment! How Feefo hated it, for the bird gave away all his secrets, and told all sorts of

27

stories about him, making him go red a dozen times a day. And at last he decided that the only thing to do was to behave nicely, and then the Cockyolly Bird couldn't say anything.

After a time he became quite a nice little goblin. He was no longer selfish and mean, and he didn't tell stories. The Cockyolly Bird got quite fond of him, and when the time came for her to go she wept bitterly.

Feefo comforted her, and told her she could stay if she wanted to, because he was fond of her too. So she stayed and was very happy.

'I'll build my next nest in your rafters, Feefo,' she said. 'But you won't take my eggs, will you?'

'Oh, *no*!' said Feefo. 'I wouldn't *dream* of doing anything so horrid!'

So you can see what a different person he was, can't you?

4. Mollie's Lovely New Umbrella

Mollie had a beautiful new umbrella on her birthday. It was green silk, and had a green handle to match, and on the end of it was a parrot's head. It really was a lovely umbrella.

Mollie was very proud of it. She wished it would rain every day for a month, then she could use it. She wanted to take it to school to show all her friends. But the sun shone, and shone, and shone, and the weather was so hot and dry that it was silly even to *think* of taking an umbrella to school.

Then one Saturday Mollie woke to see a stormy sky. The sun stayed behind the clouds, and the wind blew from the west.

'It looks like rain today,' said Mollie's father at breakfast-time.

'Oh, I wish it was yesterday,' said Mollie. 'Then I could have taken my umbrella to school.'

'Look! There's the rain, sure enough!' said Daddy. 'I *am* glad to see it. The garden has got so very dry and dusty, and all my pet plants are dying.'

Mollie stood at the window and watched the rain pouring down. How she wished it was a school-day, then she could have used her umbrella for the first time.

'Mummy,' she said, 'may I go for a walk this morning?'

'What, in the rain!' said her mother, astonished. 'Oh, no, Mollie, you'll get wet.'

'But, Mummy, I can take my new umbrella,' said Mollie. 'And I'll put on my goloshes and my mackintosh too. Oh, do let me! I do so want to use my lovely new umbrella!'

'Well, you may go if you want to,' said Mummy, smiling. 'You can take a message for me to old Mrs. Brown, the other side of the wood.'

'Oh, that *will* be a nice long walk!' said Mollie, pleased. 'I can hold my new umbrella up all the way!'

She put on her goloshes, her mackintosh, and her hat. Then, stuffing her mother's note in her pocket, she fetched her new green umbrella. She put it up, and proudly walked out into the rain.

The umbrella was really beautiful. It kept every drop of rain off, and it looked very pretty indeed. Mollie wished she could meet a hundred people so that they might see her umbrella.

But she didn't meet anyone at all. She was so sorry, because it did seem a pity that no one should see her lovely umbrella. She went right through the wood, and when she felt the raindrops pattering off the trees she was delighted.

Mrs. Brown wasn't at home, so Mollie couldn't even show *her* the umbrella. It was most disappointing. She slipped the note into the letter-box, and then turned to go back home. On her way through the wood she thought that it would be rather a good idea to go where the trees were thicker, for then she would hear heaps of raindrops pattering on her umbrella.

But she found that the trees sheltered her from the rain, and hardly any drops fell at all. The ground beneath was almost dry. So she turned to go back to the right path.

And then she found that she had lost her way! She went this way and that, but she *couldn't* seem to find the path. She began to feel frightened.

'Oh, what a horrid morning this is, after all!' she said. 'No one has seen my lovely umbrella, and now I have lost my way.'

Just as she said that she heard a little voice somewhere near by saying:

'Look! That little girl has got a lovely umbrella! That would do nicely!'

Mollie turned and saw four little fairies in green. They ran towards her, smiling. She was most astonished, for although she believed in fairies she had never seen any.

'Could you lend us your umbrella for a minute?' asked the first fairy.

'Why?' asked Mollie. 'Haven't you got any?'

'Oh, yes, plenty,' said the fairies. 'But we haven't got them with us. It isn't for ourselves we want it, but for the Queen. She is coming here in her carriage in a moment or two, and it's raining rather hard. We didn't think of bringing an umbrella – the weather has been so fine for weeks – and we are afraid she will get wet when she steps out of her carriage and walks to the pixie ribbon-shop. It isn't more than a few steps, but we shouldn't like the darling to get wet.'

'The pixie who keeps the ribbon-shop lent her umbrella to a goblin six weeks ago, and he hasn't returned it,' said another fairy. 'And all the other folk who live near by have got such dreadful old umbrellas, we really couldn't use those!'

'Then suddenly we saw yours,' said the first fairy. 'And it looked so new and beautiful that we thought it would be just the thing for the Queen!'

'It is rather a nice one, isn't it?' said Mollie, delighted. 'Of course, I'll lend it to you. But do you think I could peep round a tree somewhere and just see the Queen when she comes?'

'Certainly,' said the fairies. So they took Mollie to a big oak tree and told her to stand behind it. She saw a queer little elfin village in a clearing, and stared at it in wonder. The pixie ribbon-shop was quite near by, and the pixie who lived there had put a piece of red carpet for the Queen to tread on.

Soon there drove up a carriage made of silver and gold, and drawn by three snow-white rabbits. The Queen stepped out, and the fairies in green went to meet her. They put up Mollie's lovely umbrella, and held it over the Queen whilst she stepped from her carriage and walked to the shop.

Mollie was too excited and pleased for words! To think that her umbrella should be nice enough for that! How lovely! What would her mother say! She stood and waited for the Queen to come out again.

After a few minutes the lovely fairy walked out of the ribbon-shop. Mollie gazed at her in delight. She was very beautiful, and her long golden hair almost touched the ground. The little green umbrella was held carefully

32

over her until she got into the carriage.

'Thank you,' said the Queen, in a silvery voice. 'What a beautiful umbrella! I do wish *I* had one like that!'

Then the carriage drove away. Mollie nearly shouted with joy to think of what the Queen had said, but she kept very quiet, for she didn't want to frighten the little folk of the village.

Soon the green fairies came hurrying up, carrying her umbrella.

'Thank you *very* much,' they said. 'The Queen was delighted. We do hope you haven't got wet.'

'Only a little,' said Mollie. 'But that doesn't matter a bit. Now would you mind showing me the path home? I'm rather lost.'

The fairies soon took her to the right path, and Mollie ran home. She burst in at the door, eager to tell her mother all that had happened.

'Why, Mollie,' said her mother, 'you're wet! Didn't you have your umbrella up all the time? I wish I hadn't let you go out now! Go and take off your coat.'

'Oh, Mummy, listen,' said Mollie. And then she told her mother all that happened. But, do you know, her mother laughed and shook her head.

'You've made that little tale up!' she said. 'Open your umbrella again and put it by the fire to dry. Don't put it away folded up wet.'

Mollie opened her umbrella without a word. She couldn't bear not to be believed. Then, as she put her open umbrella down by the fire, she saw something that made her cry out in wonder – for neatly emblazoned on the green silk cover was a golden crown!

'Look!' she said. 'That's what queens and kings have on their clothes and carriages and things, isn't it, Mummy? Well, the Queen's put a crown on *my* umbrella – to show she liked it, I expect. Oh, Mummy, you'll believe me now, won't you?'

And her mother couldn't very well do anything else, could she?

5. The Elf who Wanted a Boat

Paul had a fine toy boat. It was painted blue, with a little red stripe, and had lovely oars, very small, both painted blue to match the boat. His uncle had given it to him for his birthday. Paul would rather have had a sailing-ship, but he was very pleased with the dear little boat.

'May I go and float it on the stream?' he asked his mother.

'Yes, dear,' she said. 'And look out for my ring, won't you?'

'Oh, Mummy, I *am* sorry you lost that!' said Paul, giving her a hug. His mother had dropped her ring into the water the last time she had walked by the stream, and had not been able to find it, though she and Paul had looked for a whole hour.

Off went Paul, carrying his little boat. He soon arrived at the stream, and launched the blue boat on the tiny ripples. It floated beautifully, and Paul was pleased with it. When he had played with it for some time he thought he would like to go and watch the rabbits in the field near by. So he tied his boat to the overhanging branch of a willow tree and left it bobbing up and down on the water.

He watched the rabbits for a long time. Then he thought he would go back and fetch his boat. So off he went to the stream again – and his boat wasn't there!

35

The string was still hanging to the branch, but the boat had gone.

'Someone's cut the string and taken it away!' thought Paul. 'Oh, what a shame! My new boat too! I wonder who it could have been. I haven't seen anyone come this way at all.'

He looked up the stream and down, but there was no one in sight.

'Perhaps the string broke itself and the boat floated away,' he suddenly thought. 'I'll look and see if it is bobbing up and down somewhere not far away, all by itself.'

He followed the stream, and looked carefully in all the little corners of the bank. No, there was no boat. It was very disappointing.

And then he suddenly saw it! It was some way ahead, floating merrily right in the very middle of the stream! Paul ran along the bank till he caught up with it, and then he stopped still in the greatest astonishment – for there was someone in it!

It was a very tiny elf, just big enough for the boat. He was rowing with the little blue oars, and as he rowed he sang a happy little song. This is what he sang:

> *I've a little boat of my own, my own,*
> *And I'm voyaging off alone, alone,*
> *Down the stream and across the pond,*
> *Away to the sea and the Big Beyond!*

Paul stared in surprise. He didn't know whether to be cross or not. How dare the elf take his birthday boat and sing a song about it as if it were his very own!

He watched the little creature rowing hard and fast. He seemed very happy indeed. Paul wondered if he should let him keep the boat.

'No, it's naughty of him to take it without asking,' he thought. 'I must call him.'

'Hi!' he shouted. 'Hi! What are you doing?'

The elf was so surprised that he nearly fell out of the boat. He stopped rowing and looked round.

'Are you calling me?' he shouted, in a tiny, silvery voice. 'What's the matter? Can't you see I'm rowing?'

'Of course I can!' said Paul. 'But why have you taken my boat? You oughtn't to take other people's things, you know. That's very wrong.'

'Oh, dear!' cried the elf in dismay. 'Is this *your* boat? Oh, I thought it was a stray one that belonged to nobody, so I took it for mine, because I've always wanted one, all my life long. And it fits me so beautifully, doesn't it?'

'Yes, but it's *my* boat,' said Paul. 'You ought to give it to me back.'

'Oh, I will!' said the elf, and he began rowing to the bank. He jumped out when he got there, and pulled the little blue boat to shore.

'That's the biggest disappointment I've ever had,' he said, with a sigh. 'I've longed and longed for a boat like this, and never had one. I made up a little song about it too. I was just going off on my adventures.'

Paul was sorry for the tiny creature. He really did look very miserable. The little boy couldn't bear to take the boat from him.

'It's all right,' he said to the elf. 'You can have it for

your own, and go adventuring in it, if you like.'

'What!' cried the elf. 'Don't you want it?'

'Well, I do want it really,' said Paul. 'But you want it more than I do, so I'll give it to you. Jump into it again, and row off while I watch you.'

'You kind boy!' cried the elf. 'You very generous boy! Oh, thank you! But do, do tell me what you'd like in exchange for it! I must give you something – I really must.'

'I don't want anything,' said Paul. 'Really I don't. Mummy wouldn't like me to take anything for being kind. She says if you're kind and you expect something back for it you're not being really kind. So, if you don't mind, I'll just give you the boat for nothing, because you badly want it.'

'But I must give you something!' cried the elf, quite upset. 'I really must! Can't you think of anything? Or isn't there something I can *do* for you?'

Paul was just going to say no, there wasn't, when a thought came into his head.

'There *is* something,' he said. 'I wonder if you really *could* do it for me. It's not for myself, but for my mother. She lost her ring in the water last week, and we couldn't find it. I suppose you couldn't get it for me?'

'Of course I could!' cried the elf, in delight. 'Easiest thing in the world! Half a minute!'

'Ho there, newt!' cried the elf. 'Go and seek for a ring that was dropped in the water. It will be hidden some- where in the mud.'

The newt disappeared under the water. Paul was most astonished that it should understand what the elf said.

38

Before he had time to wonder very long, the newt came back. It popped its head above the water again, and in its mouth was – what do you think? Yes, you're right – the ring! It was a diamond one, and it shone and sparkled brightly in the sunshine. The elf got into the little boat, rowed to the newt, and took the ring from its mouth.

He patted the creature on the nose, and thanked it. It vanished beneath the water, and the elf rowed back to the bank.

'Here you are,' he said, and gave Paul the ring. 'Now are you sure you wouldn't like me to do anything else for you?'

'Quite, thank you,' said Paul. 'Row down the stream, little elf, and have a good time in my boat!'

'Thank you so much!' said the elf, happily. He headed down the stream again, and rowed off quickly, singing the little song in his high, silvery voice. Paul watched till he was out of sight. Then he ran home, wondering what his mother would say when he showed her the ring.

She couldn't believe her eyes at first. She took it from Paul and looked and looked at it.

'Oh, Paul!' she said. 'My lovely ring! You've found it for me! You clever, clever boy! How glad I am!'

'*I* didn't find it,' said Paul, and he told his mother all that had happened. She *was* astonished.

'So you gave the elf your birthday boat!' she said. 'You're a nice boy, Paul. It is good to be unselfish.'

And do you know what his mother did? She was so pleased to have her beautiful ring back that she went straight to the toyshop and bought a big sailing-ship for

Paul, the very one he had always longed to have!

'So I've got the ship, after all!' cried Paul, when he saw it. 'Oh, I really am the luckiest boy in the world!'

But I think he deserved it, don't you?

6. *The Donkey that Ran Away*

There was once a donkey who had a very kind master. He had oats and carrots every day, and in the summertime a field of good green grass all to himself. He should have been very happy, but he wasn't.

'It's such a nuisance to have to pull my master's cart to market and back,' thought the donkey. 'Why can't I be left in peace in my field? Why should I have to work?'

The more he thought about this the more discontented he became. And at last he made up his mind to run away.

'I'll go and find another master,' he thought, 'one who will let me lie in a nice sunny field all day long, and do just what I like.'

So that night he jumped over the gate and ran away. He raced down the lane and up the hill and down into the next valley. Then he found a wide road, and trotted along it for miles. When day was breaking he found himself in a large town, and there was not a field to be seen anywhere.

The donkey was astonished. He had never seen a big town before, for his own market-town was very small. He ran along the streets, looking about him, and wondering where he could get food.

At last he came to a shop where carrots, cabbages,

onions, apples, and plums were all spread out in baskets. The donkey stopped and sniffed.

'Ha!' he thought. 'This is the place for me! I'll just have my breakfast here!'

So he trotted up to the baskets, and began to crunch up apples and carrots. As soon as the shopman saw what he was doing he came rushing out, and beat him with a stick.

'Stop eating my goods, you wicked donkey!' he cried. The donkey was surprised, for no one had ever spoken crossly to him before. He was even more surprised to feel the stick on his back, and he brayed in fright.

The shopman put a halter round his neck, and tied him up in a yard at the back of the shop. There the donkey was left for some hours, and though he tried his best to get away he could not.

After a long time the shopman came back and led the donkey to a cart, where he quickly harnessed him.

'You robbed me of two baskets of carrots and apples, and now you can draw my cart to pay for your breakfast!' said the man sternly.

The donkey stood quite still, and wouldn't move a foot when the man called to him to trot out of the yard. Then thwack! the stick came down again, and the donkey started forward with a jerk. Thwack!

'Oh, my!' thought the startled donkey. 'I must drag this cart wherever this man wants me to, or I shall feel that horrid stick again! I shan't stay with *this* master! He is worse than the last one!'

Off he trotted out of the yard, and the greengrocer drove him to all his customers, delivering his goods at the door. The donkey was tired and hungry long before he was back in the yard.

The man gave him a feed and a drink of water. Then he put him in a shed for the night. When he had gone the donkey pushed the door with his head. He had made up his mind to run away at once. He would go and find a much kinder master, one who would pet him and give him a nice green field for himself.

He soon had the door open. He trotted out, made for the yard gate, and leapt over it. Then down the road he went as fast as ever he could. He ran and ran until he came to green fields again. He chose one that seemed quiet, without any sheep or cows in, and entered it. Then he lay down by the hedge.

Just near by was a gipsy camp. One of the gipsies heard the sound of hoofs, and looked out to see what made the noise. He was afraid that one of his donkeys was running off. By the light of the moon he saw another donkey, not his own, come running into the field all alone. In a trice he was out of the van, and ran to catch it.

The donkey felt a heavy hand on his neck, and a rope was quickly thrown over his head. He was dragged to his feet, and led to the camp. There he was tightly tied up till the morning.

When the gipsy looked at him at daybreak he was pleased. Here was a strong young donkey, well-kept and sturdy! Just what he wanted for his heaviest van! He would go off straightway before anyone came to inquire if he had seen a lost donkey.

So very quickly the camp got ready to move. The

other donkeys were harnessed to their carts, and the stray one was put to pull the biggest and heaviest van of all. How angry he was! But no matter how he kicked or brayed, he could not get away. All he got was a shower of blows that hurt him much more than the stick that the greengrocer had used.

'This master is worse than the last!' thought the donkey in despair. 'Oh, I must get away quickly!'

But the gipsies watched him too well for him to escape. When he was not drawing the van he was tied up, and day after day the poor donkey had to drag the heavy van miles along the roads. He grew thin, for he was not fed well, and he was very unhappy indeed.

'Why did I ever leave my first master?' he thought to himself. 'He was so kind. I had plenty to eat. I had a green field to lie down in. I had hardly any work to do. How I would love to work for my first master again! He didn't hit me. He didn't starve me. I didn't know how lucky I was then.'

The weeks went by and the poor donkey grew more and more unhappy. He had tried to escape once, but had been caught and well beaten. He thought that he would never be able to get away. He wished even that he could go back to his second master, the greengrocer, who at least fed him well, and gave him a shed to sleep in.

Then one day he came to the little market-town to which he had often taken his first master. The donkey knew it at once, and looked round in pleasure. How he wished he could see his kind master there!

The gipsy vans went down the road that led to his first

master's house. The donkey felt excited. They came to the house – and in the garden was the kind master himself!

The donkey was mad with joy. He brayed loudly, and then took to his heels, galloping up to the front gate and up the drive with the van behind him, swaying and swinging from side to side. The gipsies shouted and called, but the donkey would not stop. He ran right up to his first master, and brayed more loudly than ever.

The man was astonished to see a donkey dragging a gipsy van in his garden. When the donkey brayed at him, and tried to nuzzle his head on to his shoulder, he looked at him in surprise.

'Why, it's old Neddy!' he cried. 'But how do you come here, Neddy? Did the gipsies steal you? Did you run away? Where did you go?'

The donkey brayed loudly. The gipsies came running up, and the man asked them about the donkey. But they said that they had bought him at the market, and the man had to believe them.

Sadly he had to let his donkey go with the gipsies down the road. The donkey himself was full of grief. He could not tell his master all that had happened. How sad he was to think he had ever run away from such a kind home!

Two nights later the donkey found that his rope was not tied tightly to the post. His heart jumped for joy, and he dragged the rope right off the post. Then, with a loud bray, he kicked his heels up into the air and galloped back to his first home. It took him many hours to get there, but just as the day was breaking he came to the gate of his old field. He leapt over it, and ran to lie down in his favourite corner, full of delight.

But what was his surprise to find *another* donkey there! At first he thought he would kick him and bite him, but he had learnt many lessons now, and after a while he lay down quietly, and went to sleep.

The master was full of astonishment to find his old donkey in the field again! He could not think how he had got there.

'What shall I do with you?' he asked. 'I have another donkey now, and I cannot keep two. But if you promise to work hard and not get bad-tempered as you used to do when I took you to market I will sell the other donkey and keep *you*, Neddy.'

Neddy brayed his loudest. He ran to the shed where the cart was kept, and stood between the shafts to show his master that he was ready for work at once.

'You have learnt your lesson!' said the man, pleased. 'You will work well for me now, I am sure, and will do your best to return my kindness to you.'

So the other donkey was sold to an old lady who wanted one for her little grandson, and Neddy was taken back by his first master. But did he grumble or sigh about his hard life? Never once!

'I have the kindest master in the world!' he told the horse in the next field. 'I cannot do enough for him! I wish he would work me three times as hard. I love pulling his cart to market each day! It's the nicest thing in my whole morning's work!'

'Ho ho!' said the old horse, wisely. 'You tell me a different story now, Neddy. Do you remember the things you used to say before you went away? What a foolish donkey you were then!'

'I am wise now!' said the donkey, and he galloped round his field as fast as ever he could.

7. *The Very Untidy Garden*

It was holiday time, and Hilda and Tommy were at home all day long. All their friends were at the seaside, but they were not going.

'Isn't it horrid!' said Hilda. 'We didn't go last year, and we're not going this year, either.'

'Well, Mummy has to work very hard for us,' said Tommy. 'And she says all the money she earns has to go for food and clothes, and there's none left for seaside holidays.'

Their mother was a nurse, and often had to go away from home for weeks at a time, nursing ill people. Their father was dead, and when their mother was away their Aunt Ellen came to look after them. She was very strict, and not very kind, so the children did not have a very good time in the holidays.

Aunt Ellen won't let us go for picnics or anything nice!' sighed Hilda. 'It's so dull to be at home all day long. Whatever can we do?'

'And we mustn't make a noise in the garden because of the old gentleman next door who is ill,' said Tommy. 'These are going to be perfectly *horrid* holidays!'

'Well, anyway, our garden is very pretty,' said Hilda, looking at the rows of gay flowers in the beds. 'I'm glad we weeded it so well, aren't you, Tommy? And all the seeds we planted have come up beautifully!'

48

'Yes,' said Tommy. 'We've got a nice garden – better than the old man's next door! Isn't it terribly weedy!'

Hilda looked over the wall. It really was a very untidy garden. There were plenty of lovely plants in it, trying their hardest to flower – but they were so choked by thistles, dandelions, nettles, and other weeds that they found it very difficult to hold their own.

'I say!' suddenly said Tommy. 'What about weeding the next-door garden, Hilda? That would be something to do, wouldn't it? And think how fine it would look when it was all nice and tidy! I hate to see those lovely flowers choked like that.'

Hilda loved gardening just as much as Tommy did, so she at once agreed.

'I suppose the old man wouldn't mind, would he?' she asked.

'Why should he?' asked Tommy. 'Anyway, he's too ill to mind. We'll just do it without saying anything to anyone. Aunt Ellen will think we're doing something quiet in our own garden. She won't guess where we are.'

The two children felt quite excited. It was a real secret, and they wanted to begin work at once. So they fetched their basket and their trowels, and an old pair of gloves to wear when pulling up the nettles, and over the wall they climbed!

They set to work. Oh, what a weedy garden it was! The children had never in their lives seen such big weeds. It was really quite difficult to pull some of them up. Before tea-time came they had cleared one small bed, and it looked lovely. The hollyhocks and snapdragons seemed very grateful, and swayed happily in the breeze.

The next day the children climbed over the wall again. They set to work on a second bed, bigger than the first one, and it took them nearly the whole of the day to make it look nice. They were pleased about their secret, and felt quite certain that nobody knew it.

But somebody *did* know it! And who do you think that somebody was? Why, the old man himself! He was getting better, and he was allowed to sit at the window of his bedroom for the first time on the day that the children had decided to weed his garden.

He saw them climb over the wall, and he frowned. Then he saw that they had trowels and baskets, and he wondered what they were going to do. Surely they couldn't be so naughty as to dig up his lovely plants?

He watched them, and to his great surprise he saw that they were carefully pulling up all the weeds! What surprising children! Who would have thought of such a thing!

'Look, Nurse,' he said, when she came into the room. 'Do you see those children in my garden? What do you think they are doing?'

'Oh, the naughty children!' said the nurse. 'They're from next door. Shall I go and send them away, Mr. Jones?'

'No, no, certainly not,' said the old man. 'Don't you see that they're weeding the garden? Isn't that extra-ordinary! I didn't think there were children in the world who could make up their minds to do a thing like that! It's very, very kind of them. Don't let them know that I have guessed their secret. I shall love to sit here and watch how they get on.'

So every day the old man sat at his window and watched Hilda and Tommy hard at work in his garden. Bit by bit they cleared all the weeds, and even tied up some of the tall hollyhocks that were in danger of being blown down. They made the garden look perfectly lovely.

'We'll weed the paths tomorrow,' said Tommy. 'Then we've done everything we *can* do, Hilda! Won't the old man be surprised!'

The next day they set to work to weed the paths, and suddenly they heard someone coming up behind them! They jumped to their feet, and – oh, dear! – it was the old gentleman himself, looking very white, and leaning on his stick.

'How do you do?' he said. 'I am very pleased to meet you.'

'W-we're quite well, th-thank you,' said the children, rather frightened. 'We were just weeding your p-path. We hope you don't mind.'

'Not at all,' said the old man. 'It's very kind of you. I have been watching you making my garden beautiful every day.'

'Oh!' said Hilda and Tommy, going red. 'We thought no one knew.'

'Then you were wrong,' said the old man.'But I can't stay out here any longer. Will you come indoors and have tea with me? There is a fine chocolate cake today.'

'We'll ask Aunt Ellen,' said Tommy. 'Thank you very much.'

They climbed over the wall. Aunt Ellen said yes, they could go, but they must first wash their hands and brush their hair. They did as they were told, and then, looking very spick and span, went politely round to the front door and rang the bell.

The nurse opened it, and led the way into the dining-room, where a lovely tea was waiting. The old man was there, and he smiled kindly at them.

They had a fine time. They were soon talking merrily to the old gentleman, telling him what fun they had had in his garden.

'But why aren't you away at the seaside, like other children?' he asked.

'Well, you see, Mummy is a nurse, and she's always away looking after other people,' explained Hilda. 'And she hasn't got enough money to send us to the seaside this year. So we are staying at home. We hadn't anything to do, so we thought of tidying up your garden.'

The old man said nothing for a long time. Then he said something so surprising that the children's breath was quite taken away.

'I have a good idea,' he said. 'My own nurse has to go home next week, and I must get another. The doctor says I must go to the seaside. I wonder if your mother could be my nurse, so that we could all go to the seaside together?'

What do you think of that? Wasn't that a wonderful idea? Hilda and Tommy thought it was, and how they hoped that it would all come true!

It did! Their mother wrote to say that she would like to nurse the old man at the seaside, and make him better;

and as for the children, well, if he really *did* like them, she would be so glad to have them with her too. So it was all settled, and one lovely sunny day Hilda and Tommy, their mother and the old gentleman all got into the train together.

'Hurrah for the seaside!' cried Tommy. 'What a good thing we thought of tidying up that garden, wasn't it, Hilda?'

'It was!' cried everyone, and off they went to the jolly blue sea.

There were once two little brownies called Flip and Flop. Flop was tall and thin, and Flip was fat and short. Flip lived in Flip Cottage, and Flop lived in Flop Cottage, and they were very fond of one another indeed.

Every morning Flip went to Flop's for a cup of cocoa, and took his morning paper with him to lend to Flop, who couldn't afford one. They drank their cocoa and nibbled chocolate biscuits, talking hard all the time.

And then one dreadful morning they quarrelled! They had never had a cross word before in all their lives, and when the quarrel came it was a very fierce one.

It began when Flip said that Flop had forgotten to put sugar in his cocoa.

'I put two big lumps in your cup,' said Flop indignantly. 'How much sweeter do you want it than that?'

'You must have put the lumps into your own cup instead of mine,' said Flip, stirring his cocoa so hard that it slopped over on to the cloth.

'There now! Look what you've done!' said Flop, banging on the table angrily. 'You've spoilt my nice clean cloth, and it was only put on this very morning!'

'Well, you shouldn't have forgotten to put sugar in my cocoa!' said Flip, banging on the table too. 'If you hadn't forgotten that I shouldn't have stirred my cocoa so hard, and it wouldn't have slopped on to your clean cloth. So it's really your own fault. You are a stupid little brownie!'

'And you are a nasty unkind one!' said Flop, banging the table so hard that his cup of cocoa jumped into the air and flew into Flip's lap, where it upset and covered him with hot cocoa.

'Ow! Ow!' yelled Flip, jumping up in pain. 'Oh, you horrid, nasty, silly, stupid brownie! Look what you've done now! You did it on purpose; I know you did!'

'Well, I didn't then,' said Flop. 'You're in a very bad temper, and perhaps the cocoa will cool you down!'

'How can hot cocoa make anyone cool?' shouted Flip. 'Do *you* want to be cool? All right, here's *my* hot cocoa to cool you then!'

And the naughty little brownie picked up his cup of cocoa and threw it all over Flop! Oh, what a to-do there was then! How they shouted and stamped!

'If you're not careful I'll make you grow as small as a mouse!' cried Flop to Flip.

'And if *you're* not careful I'll make you grow as tall as a lamp-post!' shouted Flip. 'Oh, you naughty fellow! I won't stay a minute longer in your house, and I'll never come and see you again!'

With that he rushed into the hall, took down hat, coat, umbrella, and gloves, slipped on goloshes and ran down the front path in a most fearful temper.

Flip was very angry indeed as he walked down the road. His little fat legs hurried along, and he frowned so hard that everyone he met stared at him in surprise, for usually he was a most good-tempered fellow.

After a while he became very cross with his hat, which

would keep slipping down over his eyes.

'It's a funny thing that my hat won't keep on properly this morning,' said Flip crossly, pushing it off his forehead for the fifth time.

Then he got cross with his goloshes, which seemed to flop, flop, flop as he walked. He looked down at them and saw that they were much too big for his feet – and then an awful thought came to him.

'Flop has put a spell on me!' he wailed. 'He said he would make me as small as a mouse, and I'm getting smaller. I must be, because my hat is too big already, and my goloshes are far too large for my feet. Oh, my! oh, my! whatever shall I do? How *wicked* of Flop! I'll never, never forgive him – never!'

He stopped and looked at himself in a mirror that hung outside a shop – and, oh, what a queer sight met his eyes! His hat was slipping down over his forehead again. his goloshes were nearly off his feet, his coat was far too long, his gloves didn't fit him at all, and as for his umbrella, it was nearly as tall as he was!

'I'm getting as small as a mouse!' said Flip dolefully. 'Oh, what a dreadful thing! What can I do about it? I'd better go to the police station and tell the policemen how wicked Flop is, and then perhaps they will fetch him and make him take this awful spell off me.'

So he walked to the police station and all the policemen laughed heartily when they saw such a queer little figure coming in.

'Don't laugh,' said Flip mournfully. 'I have a terrible spell on me, put there by that wicked fellow Flop.'

'But I thought you and Flop were such friends!' said the policemen in surprise.

'We're enemies now,' said Flip. 'I'll never be friends again with him. He's put a spell on me to make me get smaller. Look, my hat is far too big already, and so is my coat. My goloshes won't keep on, and my gloves are no use at all. As for my umbrella, it's nearly as tall as I am. Fetch Flop at once and put him in prison for doing this wicked thing to me!'

The biggest policeman began to write in a book. When he had written down all that Flip had said he told two more policemen to go and fetch Flop.

Off they went. They soon arrived at Flop's cottage, and he was very much frightened when he saw them.

'You've put a spell on Flip and made him go small,' said one of the policemen sternly.

'Oh, I haven't!' said Flop in dismay. 'I haven't, really. I know I said I would if he wasn't careful, but I didn't mean it really, you know. And besides, he said he would put a spell on me to make me grow as tall as a lamp-post!'

'No more talking,' said the policeman. 'You must come along with us. Put on your things and hurry up.'

Flop was terribly upset. He went into his little hall, put on hat, coat, gloves, and goloshes, and took an umbrella from the stand. Then he walked down the front path with the two big policemen.

Now he hadn't gone very far when he began to limp, and he looked down at his feet.

'Good gracious!' he cried. 'Look at my goloshes! They are much too small for me! My feet must be growing!

and, oh, my! look at my coat! It's shrunk almost to my neck! I must be growing as tall as a lamp-post! Oh, dear, oh, dear! I believe that wicked brownie Flip has put *his* spell on me! I think he's making me grow as tall as a lamp-post! All my things fitted me yesterday, and now today they are much too small!'

The policemen looked at him. He certainly looked rather queer. His hat was far too small and was perched right on the top of his head. His goloshes were splitting in half. His coat was bursting its buttons and was half-way to his neck instead of reaching his knees. His gloves were splitting too, and as for his umbrella it looked just like a toy one.

'He does look rather funny,' whispered one policeman to another. 'Do you really think they've put spells on one another?'

'They must have,' the other policeman whispered back. 'Come on, let's take him to Flip and see what they say to one another.'

At last Flop arrived at the police station and was taken to the room where Flip was sitting, looking very small indeed in his big clothes.

'You wicked fellow!' he cried, as soon as he saw Flop. 'Take this small spell off me at once. I'm quite small enough in the ordinary way without being made any smaller!'

Then he suddenly stopped and looked closely at Flop in surprise.

'What have you been doing, Flop?' he asked in aston- ishment. 'You do look funny.'

'What have I been doing!' cried Flop in a rage. 'I like

58

that! You know very well that you've put a spell on me and made me grow bigger, as you said you would! So now all my clothes are splitting because they are too small.'

'*I* haven't put any spell on you,' said Flip in surprise. 'Really I haven't, Flop. I didn't mean what I said, you know. It's you who have put a spell on me and made me grow so small that all my clothes are too large.'

The biggest policeman looked hard at Flip and Flop. He knew them very well indeed.

'Do you know,' he said, 'I don't think Flip has grown any smaller, or Flop any larger. It's just that your clothes are too big for you, or too small. Have you got on your right coats and hats and goloshes?'

Flip jumped up and took off his coat. He looked inside the collar – and, oh, what *do* you think? He had got Flop's coat on, for there inside was the name – FLOP! Then Flip looked at his hat, and sure enough it was Flop's. The gloves were Flop's too, and so were the goloshes, and the umbrella had a neat little tab inside with FLOP written on it too.

'Oh, Flop,' said Flip in a very small voice, 'I was in such a hurry when I left your cottage that I must have put on your things by mistake and taken your umbrella. Of course they were all much too big for me, but I didn't notice it at first. When I found the hat was slipping over my forehead and the goloshes were flopping off, I at once thought I was getting smaller, and that you had put a spell on me. I didn't think I had taken the wrong clothes.'

'So you left me yours!' cried Flop. 'And when I put

them on and found them all too small for me I thought you had done as you said and put a spell on me to make me get larger. I didn't guess *I* had the wrong clothes on! Quick, let's change back, and see if we are really our ordinary size.'

So they changed hats, coats, gloves, goloshes, and umbrellas, and, lo and behold they fitted perfectly! So Flip wasn't really any smaller and Flop wasn't really any larger. They had just made a silly mistake!

They looked at one another in shame! How dreadful to quarrel like that and make such a fuss about nothing. Then suddenly the biggest policeman began to laugh

'Ha ha ha!' he roared. 'He he he! Ho ho ho! This is the funniest thing I've ever heard of! Ha ha ha!'

'Ha ha, ho ho!' roared all the other policemen. 'Flip and Flop, go home again and don't quarrel any more! You're just a pair of sillies!'

The two brownies shook hands very solemnly, then they hugged one another hard. After that they began to laugh too, and out of the police station they went, still laughing, and they didn't stop till they reached Flop's cottage.

'Come in and have a nice cup of cocoa,' said Flop. 'We'll never quarrel again, Flip, will we?'

'No,' said Flip. 'We certainly won't.'

And they never did!

9. The Little Red Shawl

There was once a little old lady who lived in a tiny cottage and knitted all day long. One day she bought some red wool, and it was such a lovely colour that she thought she would make it into a little red shawl.

So she set to work and began. She knitted hard for many weeks, and at last the shawl was finished. It was very beautiful, and there was not a mistake in it.

On the day that it was finished a carriage and pair drove up the road past the little old lady's cottage. In the carriage sat the Queen of that land, a lovely lady, and as good as she was beautiful. She wore a pretty frock, but no coat; and just as she passed the little old lady's cottage she sneezed three times.

'Dear me!' she said. 'How foolish I was not to wear a coat this afternoon. I know I shall catch a cold!'

Now the little old lady had very sharp ears, and she heard every word that the Queen said. In a trice she caught up the little red shawl and ran out into the street. The carriage had just passed, but the old lady called after it.

'Coachman! Coachman! Stop, please!'

The coachman heard her voice and turned his head in surprise. The Queen heard the shouting too, and when she saw that it was a little old lady she told the coachman to stop and see what was the matter.

So the carriage stopped and the old lady trotted up, all out of breath, but as pleased as punch.

'Your Majesty,' she said. 'You are cold. Here is a little red shawl that I have just finished making. Please accept it and wear it today in your carriage.'

'Thank you very much,' said the Queen, and she took it and wrapped it round her shoulders. 'How beautifully warm it is! I shall love to wear it. Now do please get into the carriage with me and come and have tea at the palace.'

Well, the little old lady could hardly believe her ears! She got her best bonnet and her best wrap and popped into the carriage beside the Queen. Then off they drove to the palace and the old lady had the time of her life eating jam sandwiches and chocolate cake with the lovely Queen.

The little red shawl was delighted to find itself round the Queen's shoulders. It wrapped her round very warmly and was very proud.

'I shall look after her and keep her from getting cold every day,' it thought. 'How lucky I am to belong to the Queen!'

The Queen loved the little red shawl. She wore it every evening, and it suited her very well. For five years she kept it, and the shawl was very happy, for it was well taken care of. It was washed every week, and whenever a tiny hole came in it it was mended carefully.

But at the end of five years the Queen looked at it and sighed.

'My dear little shawl,' she said, 'I am afraid I must part with you. You are really getting too old for me to wear. There are so many thin places in you that soon you will be nothing but holes! I must give you away.'

How upset the shawl was to hear that! It looked at itself in the glass and sure enough it looked very old, and certainly not fit to be round the shoulders of the Queen, who was lovelier than ever.

The next week the Queen's old nurse came to stay, and the Queen thought that it would be a good idea to give the shawl to her, for she had nothing but a black wrap that had no warmth in it at all – and even though the little red shawl was old, it was still very warm to the shoulders.

So the old nurse took the shawl and had it for her own. She wore it every day, and when she left the palace she took it with her. At first the shawl missed the Queen very much, but it soon became fond of the old nurse. She had many friends who admired the shawl and thought her lucky to have one that the Queen herself had worn.

The shawl was still washed carefully every week and mended. But the old nurse had not got very good eye-sight, so the darns were rather ugly, and soon the shawl looked patchy, with darns of pink, blue, and green here and there.

Then one day the nurse went to see a woman who had just got a new little baby of her own. The woman was very poor and she had no shawl for the tiny little girl who lay in her cot as good as gold.

'You must have my shawl,' said the old nurse. 'Take care of it, for the Queen herself gave it to me. Wrap it round the baby and it will keep her beautifully warm.'

So once again the shawl changed hands, and became

the baby's wrap. Every day the little creature was wrapped warmly in it, and when the shawl felt tiny hands pulling at it it was glad. The baby loved the old shawl, and thought it was a beautiful colour.

The shawl was happy. It liked to be loved, and it always rejoiced when the mother wrapped it tightly round the baby's warm little body. But soon the little girl grew up, and when she was three years old the mother put the shawl into a cupboard and left it hanging there.

It was very dirty, for it had only once been washed by the mother, and it was so full of holes that there was no use in mending it. It hung in the cupboard for weeks and weeks, till one day an old beggar-woman came to the door with some plants to sell.

'I don't want any plants,' said the mother. 'I have no money to spend.'

'Now see this beautiful plant, all in blossom,' said the beggar-woman. 'Have you no old coat or old shawl you could give me? You shall have this plant in exchange.'

The mother suddenly remembered the little red shawl hanging in the cupboard, and she ran to fetch it. The shawl felt itself taken down from its peg and it wondered if it was going to wrap the little girl round again. It had been very unhappy and lonely for weeks, for no one had taken any notice of it at all.

'Here you are,' said the mother. 'You can have this old shawl, if you like. Give me the plant in exchange.'

The beggar-woman took the shawl and put it round her shoulders. Then she gave the mother the plant and went off down the path.

The shawl was glad to be round someone again. It

hugged the beggar-woman tightly, and she was glad of the warmth. She pulled it more closely round her and the shawl could have sung for joy. At last some one wanted it again!

For six months in wind and rain the beggar-woman wore the shawl. It was soaked with rain, and scorched with the sun, but it was happy because the beggar-woman loved it.

Then one day someone gave the woman a fine coat with a fur collar. She threw off the shawl, and put on the coat. How proud she was! She didn't give another thought to the shawl, but went on her way singing. The shawl was left in a ditch, and it lay there unheeded for weeks.

It was very sad. It remembered the days when the Queen had worn it, and thought of all the grand people who had admired it. It thought of the old nurse and how carefully she had washed it each week, just as the Queen had done. It thought of the little baby it had warmed day after day, and last of all it thought of the beggar-woman who had worn it in all weathers.

'Now nobody wants me,' sighed the shawl as it lay forgotten in the ditch.

Now in the field near by was a scarecrow. He wore an old top hat, a ragged coat and a pair of old breeches. He stood out there in the middle of the field, and frightened the crows and jackdaws who came hopping round. He was a merry fellow, and often sang a song as he stood doing his work. He was only made of beansticks with a turnip for a head, but he flapped about in the wind as lively as could be.

One day a tramp came by and saw the old scarecrow standing there, flapping its coat in the wind.

'That coat's better than mine,' said the tramp, and he popped into the field, took off the scarecrow's coat and made off with it. Then how funny the old scarecrow looked! He had only a hat and his breeches, and he felt very cold indeed.

He shivered and shook in the wind, for he missed the coat very much. Then he began to sneeze, and he nearly sneezed his turnip head off.

'Oh, my, oh, my!' he groaned. 'I shall catch a dreadful cold; I know I shall!'

The little red shawl peeped through the hedge and saw him. It felt very sorry for the scarecrow, and wished that it was near enough to talk to him. Then suddenly a splendid idea came to the shawl.

'Ho, wind!' said the shawl. 'Blow me into the field, please.'

So the wind blew the shawl into the field, and it lay there near the scarecrow.

'Oh, little red shawl!' cried the scarecrow. 'Come a little nearer! If only you could put yourself round my shoulders it would be fine.'

But the little red shawl couldn't do that, and the wind couldn't seem to manage it either. Then one morning the farmer came into his field and saw that the scarecrow had lost his coat. He spied the shawl near by and in a trice he picked it up and wrapped it round the scarecrow's shoulders.

How happy they both were! The shawl was full of joy to warm someone again, and the scarecrow no

66

longer shivered and shook in the breeze. He was as warm as toast.

'Tell me about you life,' said the scarecrow.

Then the shawl began to tell its adventures, just as they were told to you, and the scarecrow listened in delight.

'But now I am happier than ever before!' said the little red shawl. 'I love you, old scarecrow, and I am sure you love me!'

'You are the most beautiful shawl in the world!' said the scarecrow. And the best of it was that the scarecrow really meant what he said.

One day, in the very middle of winter, the elf Hickory-ho looked out of the hollow tree in which he had slept for the night. Snow lay on the ground, and the frost tried to bite Hickory's nose. He didn't like it at all, for he was very cold indeed.

'Ooh!' said Hickory-ho, rubbing his hands together. 'I wish I had a warmer suit. This one of mine is only made of red creeper leaves, and though it looks warm it isn't.'

Just then a robin flew down near by with all its feathers puffed out, and Hickory looked at it.

'Now if only I had a fine suit of feathers like that robin I'd be as warm as toast,' said the elf. 'Hi, robin! Can you spare me a few feathers?'

'How many?' asked the robin.

'Oh, about twenty,' said Hickory.

'I should think *not*!' said the robin, indignantly. 'Why, I should freeze to death if I began to give twenty feathers to every stupid little elf that asked me!'

'Nasty thing!' said Hickory-ho, and he made a face at the robin.

The day got colder and colder, and Hickory shivered and shook. He made up his mind that he would get a suit of feathers *somehow*, and he sat in his hollow tree and thought and thought. Then a curious idea came to him,

68

and he leapt out of the tree and went to a little shop near by.

It was kept by a pixie who sold nothing but china – china plates, cups, and saucers; china jugs; china teapots and hot-water jugs; and all kinds of china ornaments.

'What do you want?' asked the pixie, when Hickory came into his shop.

'Have you such a thing as a china cat you could lend me?' asked Hickory. 'I can't buy it, for I have no money; but if you would be kind enough to lend it to me I would be very grateful.'

The pixie was kind-hearted, so he lent a big white china cat to the elf, who ran off with it. Hickory-ho went to a row of houses he knew, and looked round carefully. No one was in sight. Not a cat was to be seen, and not a bird either. Hickory quickly stood the china cat on the grass, and then began to sing a song at the top of his voice. The song was made up of curious words, and soon all the robins, starlings, thrushes, blackbirds, sparrows, chaffinches round about came flying down to see what the matter was.

'What are you doing?' asked a thrush. 'And what is that thing you are singing to?'

Then Hickory-ho told a very naughty story. 'Don't you remember the big white cat who used to eat up your nestlings in the springtime?' he asked. 'Well, this is the cat. I am a wonderful elf, and I can change cats into china by using a powerful spell. I have changed that white cat into china, as you see, and it can never do you or your nestlings any harm again.'

Well, the birds thought this was wonderful. They all began talking at the tops of their voices, and the starlings talked the most loudly.

'There's a horrid black cat that lives at Number 17,' said one starling. 'I do wish he could be changed into china too. He caught my cousin yesterday and ate him.'

'And there's a very sly tabby at Number 6,' said another starling, loudly. 'He's a great nuisance, I can tell you.'

'At Number 20 there's a fine bird-table,' said a robin, in a shrill voice. 'But no one dares to go near it because of the cat at Number 19, who sits underneath the table and waits till we fly down. Then he jumps out and catches us. If ever a cat deserved to be turned into china I'm sure it's that one.'

'Well, what about the Persian cat at Number 3?' asked the blackbird. 'He ate every one of my babies last spring.'

'What a pity we can't get these cat enemies of ours changed into china,' sighed the chaffinch. 'I suppose you can't do that for us, can you, elf?'

'Why, certainly, certainly,' said Hickory-ho. 'It's as easy as anything.'

'Good gracious!' cried all the birds. 'Would you believe it! What a wonderful elf you are! Well, when will you do this for us?'

'As soon as you like,' said Hickory-ho. 'But you must pay me for it, you know.'

'We have no money,' said the chaffinch. 'We can't pay you.'

'I don't want money,' said the elf. 'You can pay me in feathers, if you like. If you each give me one feather that will quite satisfy me.'

Well, the birds didn't mind that at all. Each of them pulled out a down feather and threw it to Hickory-ho. He picked them all up eagerly and said thank you.

'Now go and change the cats into china for us, just like that one you have there,' said the blackbird.

But at that moment it began to snow, and the elf said they would have to wait for the morning. They flew away, and Hickory-ho found a cosy place under a lilac bush. He sat there with the china cat, and began to make himself a suit with the feathers. Oh, what a fine suit that was!

'Black, brown, red, speckly, and shiny feathers!' said Hickory. 'How smart I shall look, and how warm I shall be! And I do believe I shall have enough to make myself a cap of feathers too!'

All that day and all that night Hickory sat and made his feathery suit. Then, when morning came, and the winter sun tried to creep out from behind the thick clouds, the elf put on his new suit and danced about in it.

'It's warm! It's warm!' he cried. 'Oh, what a lucky elf I am! How silly those birds were to believe my story about the china cat! I must creep away from this garden before they come flying down to tell me to keep my word.'

He put the china cat under his arm, and crept out from beneath the lilac bush. He was just walking across the snowy grass when something happened.

A great black cat saw him, and thought he was a bird, for he was quite hidden in his feathery suit and cap. In a trice the cat leapt at him, and poor Hickory-ho found himself lying on his back in the snow. He yelled and shouted, and all the birds around flew down to see who was caught.

'Why it's the elf who said he could change cats into china!' they said. 'Go on, elf, change this cat into china! You will soon be free from his claws then!'

'Oh, beat him off with your wings!' cried Hickory. 'I can't change cats into china. That was all a naughty story. Oh, forgive me, and chase the cat away!'

But the birds wouldn't, for they were very angry to hear that the elf had deceived them so. They flew away and left him to the cat.

'Change cats into china, indeed!' said the cat, who had heard everything. 'I'll teach you to say things like that!'

With his sharp claws he tore Hickory's new feather suit into rags, and ate up every feather. He scratched the elf on the hands, and clawed off both his shoes. Then he broke the china cat and ran off laughing.

Hickory stood up, crying bitterly. His new suit was gone, his shoes were no use, and the china cat was broken. What a silly he had been!

'I'll never, never play such naughty tricks again!' he sobbed. 'Oh, why was I so bad? Now I shall have to pay the pixie for his broken china cat, and I haven't any money! And my suit is gone, and I must have some new shoes.'

'Ha ha ha!' laughed all the birds around. 'It serves you

right, you naughty little elf. Get out of this garden before we peck you!'

So off went Hickory-ho with the bits of the china cat under his arm. The pixie at the shop made him work very hard to make up for breaking his china – and to Hickory's great surprise he wasn't cold any more!

'Ah, hard work is the best hot-water bottle!' said the pixie in the china shop. 'Come along, Hickory. Sweep out the shop now. That will make you warmer still!'

And it did!

There was once a mean little gnome called Niggle. He kept hens and sold his eggs to the folk of Acorn Town. He would never give any away, no matter how many he had – he meant to be rich, you see.

Now one day the chief of Acorn Town, Bron the brownie, decided to give a party. But he said he wouldn't ask Niggle the gnome because he was so very mean. So when the invitation cards were sent out Niggle didn't get one.

He was very much surprised, and he asked his neighbour Waitabit if he knew why.

'Yes,' said Waitabit, with a sly grin. 'Bron says you are mean, so he won't ask you.'

Well, Niggle was very much upset to hear that. He sat down on his stool and wondered what to do.

'I had better give some of my eggs away to old Dame Ring-a-rose,' he decided. 'Then when Bron hears I have been generous, he will ask me to his party.'

But do you know what that horrid little gnome did? Why, he had six eggs that he *knew* were bad, and it was those he packed into a little basket for old Dame Ring-a-rose! He wasn't going to give her good eggs, not he!

He set off and knocked at her door. The old dame was ill in bed and the little maid came.

'Please give these eggs to Dame Ring-a-rose with my

74

best wishes,' said Niggle, and he handed the basket to the surprised maid.

Now, as he was going home, who should he meet but Bron the brownie.

'Good morning,' said Bron, with his smallest smile. 'Where have you been?'

'Oh,' said Niggle, 'I heard poor old Dame Ring-a-rose was ill, so I have just given her six of my best eggs.'

Bron was most surprised. He stared at Niggle and wondered if perhaps the folk of Acorn Town had been telling untruths about him. Then he put his hand in his pocket and pulled out a card.

'You must come to my party,' he said. 'It's tomorrow, at three o'clock.'

'Oh, thank you,' said Niggle, and he ran off in delight.

Old Dame Ring-a-rose was most astonished when she heard that the eggs were from Niggle.

'Now what a pity he chose today to send me eggs!' she said. 'You know, the doctor says I mustn't eat any this week at all. What shall we do with them? Oh, you might run round to Mother Tick-tock, Maryann, and give her the basket of eggs. She has so many children that I'm sure she will be glad of them.'

So the eggs were taken round to Mother Tick-tock. But she was just going away to the seaside with her children, and really she didn't want the eggs at all. She popped them into the cupboard and wondered what to do with them.

'I know!' she said. 'I'll take them to Mr. Twinkle. He's been ill and will be glad of them.'

75

So she popped round to Mr. Twinkle and left them on his front doorstep. When he found them there he looked at the message with them, and thought it was very kind of Mother Tick-tock to send them to him.

'But, dear me, what a lot of eggs I've got!' he thought, as he opened his larder door. 'There's a dozen that Skippity sent, and a dozen I got from the farm, and six Mrs. Dumpy brought me this morning. These will go bad before I can eat them. Now what in the world can I do with them?'

He sat down to think, and soon he had a good idea.

'Bron is giving a party tomorrow,' he said, 'so he will be having lots of tarts and cakes and custards. His cook will be needing as many eggs as she can get. I'll just take these to her.'

So off he went and gave them to Bron's cook, who was very pleased with them indeed.

'I've just one more custard to make in this little blue dish,' she said, 'and I hadn't quite enough eggs. Thank you so much, Mr. Twinkle.'

Next day was the day of the party. All the folk of Acorn Town went to it, even Mother Tick-tock who had meant to go to the seaside with her children, but who had missed the train at the last minute. She made up her mind to go away the next day instead, and she and all her children went to Bron's party. Niggle was there too, and how he enjoyed himself!

When tea-time came what a spread there was! Chocolate buns, ginger biscuits, iced cakes, coco-nut fingers, red jelly and yellow jelly, egg custards, and creamy trifles.

Niggle sat down opposite an iced cake and a custard pudding, two of the things he liked best of all. He ate a great deal of the cake and then he helped himself to quite half of the custard pudding. It was in a blue dish and looked very nice indeed.

Niggle took a big spoonful. It tasted rather funny, but he took another, and another. He thought that perhaps it was having so much iced cake first that made the custard taste queer.

But before he had finished his plateful he began to feel very ill. He turned a bright yellow and groaned loudly.

'Niggle's ill! Niggle's ill!' cried everyone. He's been greedy and eaten too much.'

'No, I haven't!' cried Niggle. 'It's that horrid custard. It's bad. Bron shouldn't put bad custard on the table.'

Bron came up and tasted the custard. It certainly *was* bad. Now how could that have happened? He called his cook and showed her the custard.

'This is made of bad eggs,' he said. 'Where did you get them from?'

'Oh, it's the custard in the blue dish, is it?' said the cook. 'Well, those eggs came from Mr. Twinkle.'

'Mr. Twinkle,' said Bron, sternly, 'how dare you bring bad eggs to me?'

'I didn't know they were bad,' said Mr. Twinkle, looking frightened. 'They were given to me by Mother Tick-tock.'

'Well, Mother Tick-tock, it isn't like you to give bad eggs to people,' said Bron.

'*I* didn't know they were bad,' said Mother Tick-tock,

indignantly. 'They were sent to me by Dame Ring-a-rose.'

'Why, Dame Ring-a-rose, how is it you sent bad eggs to Mother Tick-tock?' asked Bron, turning to the old dame, who was leaning on her stick. She had only got up from bed that morning.

The eggs were given to me by Niggle the gnome,' said Dame Ring-a-rose, 'and he knows well enough if they were bad or not. It isn't like Niggle to give good eggs away, and that we *all* know!'

Everyone looked at Niggle, whose yellow face had suddenly turned very red. He hung his head and said nothing.

'So you gave old Dame Ring-a-rose six bad eggs in order that I might think you were not mean and would give you an invitation to my party,' said Bron. 'Well, you are well punished, Niggle. Your bad eggs were made into a custard pudding and you have eaten them. That is as it should be. You can go home.'

Poor Niggle crept home and went to bed. He had to have the doctor, and by the time he was better again the doctor's bill was very big indeed.

'Oh dear,' sighed Niggle when he saw it. 'It is very expensive to be mean; there's no doubt of that. I think I will turn over a new leaf and try to be kind instead.'

He did; and now if you go to Acorn Town and ask who is the kindest person there, I shouldn't be at all surprised if you are told – 'Why, Niggle!'

Tinkle was a pixie, and he lived with his mother in Daffodil Cottage just at the end of Twiddle Village. He was a merry little fellow, but, oh, dear me! what a dreadful memory he had.

'Goodness, Tinkle!' his mother said, quite twenty times a day, 'do you ever remember *any*thing? Things seem to go in at one ear and out at the other.'

Tinkle did the silliest things. He would make the tea for breakfast and forget to put the tea in. He would put salt in his cocoa and sugar in his egg. Once he put his gloves on his feet, and his shoes on his hands; so you can see what a terribly bad memory he had.

Of course he didn't really *try* to think. He had very good brains, but he didn't use them. Then one day he did something that made his mother feel quite upset.

He went to take the dog out for a walk. He saw some fine berries in a field, and he tied the dog to a post whilst he picked them. He didn't notice that a fine fat cow was tied near by too. The farmer who owned it had gone into a cottage just near, and left his cow outside for a moment.

When Tinkle had eaten the berries, he went to the post, untied the string, and led off what he thought was his dog – but he had untied the wrong animal – and it was the great cow that followed him!

79

Tinkle didn't notice anything at all. He went on towards his home, and when he got there he took the cow indoors and tried to make it get into his dog's basket.

'Tinkle! Tinkle! Whatever have you brought that great cow indoors for?' shouted his mother in amazement. 'Take it out at once! Oh, my goodness, whatever will you do next! You've frightened me nearly to death! A cow in my nice clean kitchen indeed! I never heard of such a thing in my life!'

'Well!' said Tinkle, looking at the cow in astonishment. 'How did that happen now? I quite thought it was the dog. No wonder it couldn't sit down in the basket.'

Tinkle's mother was really quite ill with the fright, and very cross too. She talked seriously to Tinkle, and he listened.

'You know, Tinkle,' she said, 'you are growing a big pixie now. You will never be any good in the world if you are so forgetful. Now, will you promise me to try and do much better?'

Tinkle's mother looked so solemn and stern that Tinkle was frightened. He began to cry, and tears rolled down his nose.

'Oh, Mother,' he said, 'I really will be better! Truly I will! I'll never forget anything again! Do forgive me and give me one more chance.'

'Now, don't cry,' said his mother. 'I will give you another chance, and I'm sure you will do better.'

Now that afternoon a parcel arrived for Tinkle's mother. In it were three beautiful cakes, lots of small buns, a box of chocolates, a tin of biscuits, and some lovely red apples.

'All this is from your Aunt Tippitty,' said Tinkle's mother, pleased. 'Isn't she a kind soul! Now, Tinkle, I'll give you a treat. You've been a good pixie today since you promised to think hard, so I'll tell you what I'll do. You shall have a party tomorrow and eat all these good things!'

'Ooh, Mother!' cried Tinkle, in delight. 'Thank you very much.'

'Sit down and write twelve invitations in your best writing,' said his mother. 'This is what you must say:

'"Please can you come to a party tomorrow at four o'clock? Don't bother to answer, but just come. With love from Tinkle."'

So Tinkle sat down and did just what he was told. His mother looked over the notes and saw that they were nicely written.

'Here are the stamps,' she said. 'Stick them on, and then you can run out and post the letters.'

Tinkle stuck on the stamps. Then he put on his hat, put the letters carefully into his pocket, and went out to the post.

He was so excited about the party! It was the first one he had ever had. When he got back home he made out a list of games to play, and set out all his toys neatly, so that his friends might see them when they came.

'Now you must help me this morning,' said his mother next day. 'You will want fourteen chairs, so you must get them from the different rooms and set them round the table. Then you must go and buy me some fresh butter.

After that you can get out your best clothes and make sure that there are no buttons missing.'

How hard Tinkle worked, and how happy he was!

'Mother!' he said, 'I've not forgotten a single thing. I'm very clever. I'm sure I shan't forget things any more. I'm quite cured.'

At three o'clock Tinkle dressed himself in his best clothes. He set the table, and how his mouth watered to see all the good things! Ooh! what a lovely party it was going to be!

At four o'clock he went to the window to see who would come first. He could see no one in the lane, and he thought that perhaps the clock was fast. Ten minutes went by, and still no one came.

'Well, your guests *are* late!' said his mother, who was busy setting out dishes of jam. 'I wonder why. Is there no one in sight yet, Tinkle?'

'No,' said Tinkle, looking rather miserable. 'Perhaps some of them couldn't come, Mother. Oh, here's some one!'

But it was only the balloon man going to sell balloons at the corner. No one else came down the road for a long time.

The clock struck half past four.

'Well, this is very queer!' said Tinkle's mother, in surprise. 'Whatever has happened to everyone?'

Tinkle was very miserable. There were all the goodies on the table and no one to eat them! His list of games to play was up on the mantelpiece, but there was no one to play them! Why didn't anyone come?

At last, when the clock struck five, and still no one had

arrived, Tinkle's mother told him to put on his hat and run to Tick-tock's to see why he hadn't come. Then he was to go to Flip's and to Gobbo's and ask them too.

So Tinkle ran off. He knocked on Tick-tock's door, and Tick-tock's aunt opened it.

'Please,' said Tinkle, 'why hasn't Tick-tock come to my party?'

'He didn't know you were having one!' said the aunt in surprise. 'He has gone to play with his cousin.'

Then Tinkle ran to Flip's and asked Flip's mother why the little pixie had not come to his party.

'What party?' said Flip's mother in surprise. 'He didn't know anything about it! He has gone to the Zoo.'

Well, that was really very surprising. That was two people who hadn't heard of the party. And Tinkle got the same reply at Gobbo's.

'Why,' said Gobbo's mother, 'Gobbo didn't know anything about your party! Did you write to him?'

'Yes,' said Tinkle.

'Well, he has gone to see his uncle,' said the mother. 'I'm very sorry.'

Tinkle ran back home, crying. He told his mother all he had done, and she was very much puzzled. 'Don't cry, Tinkle,' she said. 'You're making your eyes so red. Where's your handkerchief?'

'I've left it in my other suit,' said Tinkle sniffing. 'I'll go and fetch it.'

He ran to fetch it. He put his hand into the pocket – and, my goodness, what was this! He pulled out of the pocket twelve letters! Tinkle stared at them in horror.

They were the invitations he had written the day before!

'Mother! Mother!' he cried, running into the kitchen with them. 'Oh, Mother! I p-p-posted my handkerchief yesterday instead of the l-l-l-letters! Oh, boo-hoo-hoo!'

'Well, of all the forgetful sillies!' cried his mother, angrily. 'And there's all this good tea wasted! Well, I've no sympathy with you, Tinkle – not a bit. You promised yesterday to use your brains, and then you go out straightway and post your handkerchief instead of your party invitations! I shan't bother with you any more. The very next time you do something silly I shall send you to Witch Think-hard, and if she doesn't teach you how to remember, well, nobody will!'

How Tinkle cried! He was so disappointed, and so angry with himself for being so silly. He had punished himself and no one else.

His mother popped a shawl over her head and ran out. Soon she was back again with some of her own friends and they all sat down to enjoy Tinkle's party cakes and buns. No one took any notice of the pixie at all. They all thought he was too silly for anything, to forget to post the invitations for his own party.

Tinkle crept off to bed. He was very unhappy. He knew quite well that his mother really *would* send him to Witch Think-hard next time.

'Well, I *must* use my brains now!' he sighed. 'I really must! What a silly I am! What a goose, what a cuckoo I am! But in future I *will* be better!'

And I'm sure you will be glad to know that he had

84

learnt his lesson at last! So many people laughed at him for posting his handkerchief that he didn't have a chance to forget his silliness, and now his brains are just as good as anyone else's!

13. The Little Prickly Family

Once upon a time all the animals in Fir Tree Wood lived together in peace and happiness. There were the rabbits and the toads, the hedgehogs and the mice, the squirrels and the moles, and many others.

Then one day King Loppy, the sandy rabbit, sat down on what he thought was a brown heap of leaves – and it was Mr. Prickles the hedgehog. He didn't like being sat on, and he stuck all his sharp spines upright, so that King Loppy jumped up with a shout of pain.

'How dare you prick the King of the Wood?' cried Loppy, standing his ears up straight in his anger. 'You did it on purpose!'

'No I didn't, really,' said Mr. Prickles. 'But it's not nice to be sat on quite so hard.'

'Well, I banish you from the wood!' said King Loppy, and he pointed with his paw towards the east, where the wood grew thinner. 'Go away at once, and take your horrid prickly family with you.'

Mr. Prickles could do nothing else but obey. So he went sadly to fetch his wife and his six prickly children. They packed up all they owned, and then the little prickly family walked out of Fir Tree Wood.

Now they hadn't been gone long when a family of red goblins came to the wood. They went to the Bluebell Dell, which was a pretty little hollow, and made

86

their home there, right in the very middle of the wood.

At first the creatures of the wood took no notice, but soon the goblins made their lives so miserable that even King Loppy vowed he would turn the goblins out.

But he couldn't! The goblins knew too much magic, and the animals were always afraid to say what they really thought for fear of being turned into mushrooms or earwigs. So they had to put up with their larders being raided each night, their firewood stolen, and their young ones frightened by the dreadful noises and ugly faces that the goblins made.

Once every month, when the moon was full, the goblins did a queer, barefoot dance in the dell. They danced round and round in the moonlight, holding hands, and singing loud songs. All the animals were kept awake, and didn't they grumble! – but not very loud, in case the red goblins heard and punished them.

'If anyone can get rid of these ugly red creatures for me, he shall be King instead of me!' declared Loppy one night. 'Our lives are a misery now, and these goblins must go!'

Well, a good many of the animals thought they would like to be King and wear the woodland crown, but try as they would, they couldn't think of a plan to make the goblins go.

Frisky the red squirrel wrote them a polite letter, and begged them to leave, but the only reply he had was to see all his nuts stolen one bright moonlight night.

Then Mowdie the mole wrote a very stern letter, and

87

said that she would get a policeman from the world of humans, and have them all locked up, if they didn't go away, but they came and laughed so loudly at her that she shivered with fright and didn't go out shopping for three days.

Then bold Mr. Hare marched right up to the goblins one day and ordered them out of the wood. He took a whip with him, and threatened to beat each goblin if they didn't obey him.

The goblins sat round and smiled. When Mr. Hare tried to use his whip he found that he couldn't move! The goblins had used magic, and he was stuck fast to the ground! Then they took his whip and whipped him with it, and tied him up to a birch-tree all night long. Loppy found him the next morning, and Mr. Hare vowed that he would never go near those horrid red goblins again!

After that no one did anything, till one day a letter came to Loppy from Mr. Prickles the hedgehog. He opened it and this is what it said:

'DEAR YOUR MAJESTY.

'I think I can get rid of the goblins for you, but I do not want to be King. I only want to be allowed to come and live in Fir Tree Wood with all my friends once more. Please let me.

'Your loving servant,
'PRICKLES'

When Loppy had read the letter he sat down and wrote an answer. This is what he said:

'DEAR MR. PRICKLES,

'You may come back here to live if you can get rid of the goblins. But I don't believe you can.

'Your loving King,
'LOPPY'

When Mr. Prickles got the letter he was overjoyed, for he felt certain he could get rid of the goblins. He looked up his calendar, and found that the next full-moon night was three nights ahead. On that night the red goblins would have their barefoot dance.

That day Mr. Prickles went to see Tibbles the pixie, who was a great friend of his.

'I want you to do something for me,' he said. 'Will you go to the red goblins in Fir Tree Wood and tell them that someone has sent you to warn them against the magic Pins and Needles?'

'Goodness!' said Tibbles, with a laugh. 'What a funny message – and whatever are the Pins and Needles?'

'Never mind about that,' said Mr. Prickles. 'You just go and give that message, there's a good pixie, and you can come back and have tea with us.'

So Tibbles set off to Bluebell Dell, and when he saw the red goblins he gave them the message.

'Someone has sent me to give you a warning,' he said, in a very solemn voice. 'You are to beware of the magic Pins and Needles.'

'Ooh!' said the goblins, looking scared. 'What are they? And what will they do? And who told you to warn us?'

'I can answer no questions,' said Tibbles, and he

walked off, leaving the goblins wondering whatever the message meant.

Now, when the night of the full moon came, Mr. Prickles and his wife and family made their way to Blue-bell Dell. The red goblins were already beginning their barefoot dance. Their shoes and stockings were laid in a neat pile under a tree.

Without being seen, Mrs. Prickles went to the pile, picked them up, and took them to the lily-pond not far off. She dropped all the shoes and stockings into the water, and then went back to her family.

'Are you all ready?' whispered Mr. Prickles. 'Then – ROLL!'

With one accord all the hedgehogs curled themselves up tightly into balls, and rolled down the dell to the bottom where the goblins were busy dancing. They rolled all among their bare feet, and soon there was a terrible shouting and crying.

'Ooh! Ooh! I've trodden on a thorn! I've trodden on a prickle! Ooh! What's this!'

The hedgehogs rolled themselves in and out, and the goblins couldn't help treading on them. The prickles ran into their bare feet, and they hopped about in pain.

'What is it? What is it?' they cried; but at that moment the moon went in, and the goblins couldn't see anything. They just went on treading on the prickly hedgehogs, and cried out in pain and fright.

Then the head goblin suddenly gave a cry of dismay, 'It must be the magic Pins and Needles! It must be! We were warned against them, we were told to beware!

Quick, put on your shoes and stockings before we get into their power!'

But the goblins couldn't find their pile of shoes and stockings – and no wonder, for they were all down at the bottom of the pond. They ran here and there looking for them, and Mr. Hedgehog and his family rolled here and there after them. How those hedgehogs enjoyed themselves!

'The Pins and Needles have taken our shoes!' cried the goblins. 'Oh, oh, what shall we do? The Pins and Needles have found us!'

'Quick!' cried the head goblin. 'We must go back to Goblin Town and buy some more shoes for our feet. We must never come back here again!'

Off the goblins ran, as fast as ever they could, and the hedgehogs rolled after them. If any goblin stopped to take breath he at once felt a prickly something on his foot, and he gave a cry of fright and ran on.

They made such a noise that all the wood animals came out to see what was the matter; and just then the moon shone out. The surprised animals saw the red goblins running for their lives, with the whole of the little prickly family of hedgehogs after them!

When the goblins were really gone, everyone crowded round the hedgehogs.

'You brave things to chase away those goblins!' cried Loppy the King. 'How could you dare to do such a thing! You are very plucky, Mr. Prickles.'

'He shall be King!' shouted the animals.

'No,' said Mr. Prickles, modestly. 'I am not great enough to be King. Loppy is far better than I am; but, please, Your Majesty, may I come back to live here, with all my prickly family?'

'Of course!' said Loppy, gladly. 'But do tell me – how did you manage to chase the goblins away, Mr. Prickles?'

'That is a secret,' said the hedgehog, and he wouldn't say another word.

Then he and all his prickly family came back to their home in the wood again and were very happy. Everyone praised them, and King Loppy had them to tea once a week, so you see he had quite forgiven Mr. Prickles for having pricked him when he sat down upon him.

As for the red goblins, they were never heard of again, but folk do say that whenever they think of that last moonlight night in Fir Tree Wood they get a funny feeling in their feet, and then they say:

'Ooh, I've got Pins and Needles!'

Have *you* ever felt that way too?

Tommy's home was poor and unhappy. His father was out of work, and his mother really couldn't get enough money to give the four children their breakfast, dinner, and tea. So Tommy often went hungry. He wasn't very old, just eight and a half, and he *did* wish he could earn something, so that he could help his mother.

When the school holidays came Mother called him to her.

'Tommy,' she said, 'you'll have to earn a little money to help me. Mr. Jones, the butcher, has just told me that he wants an errand-boy at his other shop, away in Hill-town. It will only be five shillings a week, but Mr. Jones says you can sleep at the shop and he will see that you are given your meals.'

'But, Mother!' said Tommy in fright, 'I shall have to stay away from home! I couldn't leave you all.'

'It will only be for a month, till school starts again,' said Mother. 'I'm sorry, dear, but that five shillings will make a lot of difference. You must go this morning, and show yourself to Mr. Brown, the manager of the shop in Hilltown, and see if you can get the work. Now wash yourself, and try to look big and smart for your age.'

Poor Tommy! How dreadful to leave his home for a whole month and go to live with people he didn't know – and do work he knew very little about, too. He was sure he would be no good at all. He went to wash himself, and put on his best pair of boots.

'That's right,' said his mother. 'Now, look, here's your lunch for today, wrapped up in this bag. And here's two-pence for your tram-fare into Hilltown. If you don't get the job, you'll have to walk back home. But do try, Tommy, dear, because we really are in a bad way at home, you know.'

The little boy said good-bye, and set off to walk to the tram. It was a long way into Hilltown, and he knew he would not get there until quite one o'clock.

'When I get there, I'll have my lunch and then go to the butcher's shop,' he decided.

When he came to the tram-lines he waited for a few minutes, and then climbed into the first tram that came. He gave the conductor his twopence, and took his ticket.

The tram was rather full, and as it went along on its journey it became even fuller. Soon there was not a single seat left inside, and people had to stand. Then an old man with grey hair got in, and he had to stand too, leaning heavily on his stick.

Tommy had been told by his mother that he should always give up his seat to an older person, if the tram was full. So he at once got up and touched the old man on the arm.

'Take my seat,' he said.

'Thank you, my boy,' said the old man, smiling at him. 'That's very kind of you indeed.'

He sat down in Tommy's place – and, oh, dear, poor Tommy remembered just too late that he had left his packet of sandwiches there! The old man hadn't seen them and had sat down heavily on them. They would be squashed quite flat, too messy to eat.

Now Tommy would have to go without his lunch. What a dreadful day this was! The little boy felt very miserable.

The long tram-ride came to an end. Tommy got up to go out, and saw that the old man was getting up too. The tram gave a lurch, and Tommy put out his hand to stop the old fellow from falling.

'Dear me, you *are* a helpful boy!' said the man with a laugh. The two got out, and the man put his hand into his pocket.

'Here's sixpence for you,' he said to Tommy. 'It's nice these days to see a boy with good manners.'

'Oh, no, thank you,' said Tommy. 'I couldn't take that just for giving up my seat!'

'Well, you'd better trot off home for your dinner then,' said the old man. 'It's nearly half past one. Where do you live?'

'In Littleton, a long way off,' said Tommy. 'I'm not going home to dinner today.'

'Well, where are you going to have it, then?' asked the man, surprised.

Tommy didn't know *what* to answer! He didn't like to tell his friend what had happened to his packet of sandwiches.

'What's the secret?' asked the old man, still more surprised to see Tommy blushing red.

'Well,' said Tommy, feeling most uncomfortable, 'I *did* bring some dinner with me, but you sat on it in the

95

tram. You didn't know it was on the seat I gave you.'

The old man laughed and laughed.

'Bless me!' he cried. 'Did anyone ever hear such a thing! Fancy my sitting down on your dinner! Well, well! That quite decides matters – you must come along and have some dinner with me!'

So off they went together, and soon came to a fine shop. The old man went in and he and Tommy sat down at a table.

'Bring the nicest dinner you've got!' said the man – and what a lovely dinner Tommy had! You should have seen the treacle pudding – why, it was simply *swimming* in treacle!

Tommy told the kind old man all about his home, and how his father had been out of work. He told him how he was going to see the butcher that afternoon and try to get a job as an errand-boy.

'But I shall have to sleep away from home for a whole month,' said Tommy sadly. 'And I've never been away from home before.'

'Dear, dear,' said his friend. 'That is certainly very sad for you. But, cheer up. *I* went away from home when I was a young lad too. I went all the way to Australia, and never saw any of my people again! Think of that! You will see all your family after a month – but I never did.'

'How horrid for you!' said Tommy. 'How long did you stay away?'

'Oh, for years and years,' said the man. 'I only came back to England last week. But when I came back I found all my brothers and sisters were dead, and that the only person I had still belonging to me was a nephew. So I set out to look for him – he lived somewhere about here, I was told; but, do you know, I've looked for a week, and can't find him. So now I'm going back to Australia again, all alone.'

Tommy was sorry for his new friend.

'What was your nephew's name?' he asked. 'Perhaps my father might know him.'

'His name was Jack Harris,' said the old man; 'but there are lots and lots of Harrises, you know.'

'Isn't it funny, *my* father's name is Jack Harris!' said Tommy. 'He can't be your Jack, of course – but wouldn't it be lovely if he was!'

'Now that's very strange,' said the man, staring at Tommy. 'Shall we go to your home and see if he *is* the same one?'

'Well, I must go to the butcher's shop,' said Tommy. 'I shall have to stay here if I get the job, but if I don't I'll take you back to my home.'

The little boy went off to the butcher, but although he tried to make himself as big and tall as possible, the butcher shook his head.

'No, my little man,' he said. 'You're much too young. I'm sorry – but I want someone bigger and stronger.'

Poor Tommy! This wasn't his lucky day. With tears in his eyes he left the shop and went to join his new friend, who was waiting at the corner for him.

'It's no good,' he said. 'I'm too small. Mother *will* be sorry. Do you mind walking all the way home with me? I haven't any money for another tram ride.'

'Well, *you* gave me your seat last time, so you must let

me give you a seat this time!' said the man, and together they ran to catch a tram. Tommy was very quiet all the way home, for he was afraid that his mother would be disappointed that he hadn't got the job in Hilltown.

He took his new friend to his home, and who should open the door but his father! And, do you know, as soon as Tommy's father saw the old man he cried out in surprise:

'Why, is this Uncle Will? You're just like the photograph we've got in our old album! But it can't be!'

'Then you *must* be my nephew!' said the old man, shaking Tommy's father by the hand. 'You're the Jack Harris I'm looking for! Well, well, well! And to think I shouldn't have found you if your little boy hadn't been kind enough to give up his seat in the tram to me this morning!'

What a lot of surprise and delight there was in Tommy's home that night! Great-uncle Will was rich, and he wanted to buy a farm in England, now that he had found his nephew.

'I shall want you all to come and live with me,' he said. 'Jack must manage the farm with me, and Tommy's mother can see after the house. Oh, what fun we'll all have together! Fancy Tommy being my great-nephew, and I sat on his lunch in the tram! Well, he doesn't need to be a butcher's boy now – he can wait till he's much older before he needs to earn his living!'

Everything came true as Great-uncle Will had planned, and soon the whole family moved to a lovely farm, where Tommy's father was happy and busy all the day long. But of all the children Tommy was

Great-uncle's favourite, because it was he who had helped to find his family for him.

'It *was* a good thing I gave up my seat in the tram!' Tommy said to himself, quite a hundred times, as he ran happily about the farm.

And it really was, wasn't it?

15. Chinky and the Soup

Chinky was a pixie, and he lived in Primrose Cottage, next door to Mother Tiptap's house. Mother Tiptap didn't like Chinky at all. He was always peering and prying, always listening over the fence, and for ever borrowing things from her.

'I do wish he'd go and live somewhere else!' she said, many a time. 'Really, he's a most unpleasant neighbour to have, and I'm sure there's no secret I've got that isn't known to Chinky. He's always listening to see what he can hear.'

But Chinky was very comfortable in Primrose Cottage. It had two rooms – a kitchen and a bedroom – and it would have been very easy for Chinky to keep them clean and neat. But he didn't – he was lazy and didn't bother.

It worried Mother Tiptap to see such an untidy place next door to her. The garden was full of rubbish, the roses grew anyhow, and the paths were full of weeds. Her own garden was beautful, and bright with flowers all the year round.

'If only someone nice, like Dame Twinkle, could come and live next door to me,' she sighed. 'But I'm sure that horrid little Chinky will never go. Look at him now, peering through a hole in the fence to see what I'm doing! Horrid little creature!'

One morning Dame Twinkle came to see her friend, Mother Tiptap, in great excitement.

'What do you think, my dear?' she said. 'I've just been to call on Mister Chippy, to give him some roses from my garden, and he has told me a wonderful spell!'

'Oh, do come in and tell me all about it!' said Mother Tiptap. 'I shall love to hear what it is.'

The two went indoors, and didn't see Chinky standing just by the gate. He had heard what Dame Twinkle had said, and his sharp little eyes gleamed.

'Ho!' he thought. 'A spell from Mister Chippy! That should be very good, for he has some wonderful magic-books, I know. I shall try and hear what that spell is.'

He saw the two old women go indoors, and he heard the door close. Soon he heard voices coming from Mother Tiptap's kitchen, and he knew that she was there with her friend.

Chinky jumped over the fence that stood between the two cottages and ran to the kitchen window, which was open at the bottom. He bent down beneath it and listened hard.

'Well, this is what Mister Chippy told me,' Dame Twinkle was saying. 'He said, "Now I know you are very fond of soup, and make a lot for Mister Twinkle, so here is a quick spell for making it."'

'Do go on,' said Mother Tiptap, in excitement.

'He said, "Fill a saucepan half full of clear water, put it on the stove, and let it boil. Then get a long carrot, throw it three times into the air, saying, 'Carrot, carrot, make me soup!' each time, and then put it into the boiling water. Then, whatever soup you wish for – onion, pea, potato, carrot, or bean soup – you will get." '

'Goodness me!' said Mother Tiptap, with a gasp. 'What a marvellous spell!'

'But wait a minute,' said Dame Twinkle. 'I must tell you this, too— But listen, what's that just outside the window? It sounded like someone sneezing.'

Mother Tiptap ran to the window, and saw Chinky, who had just sneezed.

'You horrid little prying creature!' she cried. 'Go home at once!'

Chinky ran home, grinning as he climbed over the fence. He had heard a spell that would give him a fine supper every night!

That afternoon he begged a carrot from Paddy-paws the rabbit, and went home with it. After tea he put a saucepan, half full of water, on his kitchen stove to boil. He fetched his carrot from the larder, threw it three times into the air, saying each time, 'Carrot, carrot, make me soup!'

Then he popped it into the boiling water and wished hard for onion soup, because he was very fond of that. And, oh, my! what a marvellous thing! The water changed in an instant to thick onion soup that sent out a most delicious smell.

The soup swelled up in the saucepan and reached the top. Before Chinky could stop it, it had run over on to the stove, and then it began to pour out in a stream! Soup, soup, soup, there was nothing but soup! It poured out of that saucepan in a torrent, and soon the kitchen floor was swimming with it.

'Ow!' yelled Chinky, as the boiling soup scalded his

toes. 'Stop it, soup!'

But it wouldn't stop. It just went on pouring out of that saucepan, and Chinky couldn't get near the stove to take the saucepan from the fire, because the soup was far too hot to walk in. Soon the soup flowed into the bedroom too, and Chinky ran before it, howling dismally. He saw his big rubber boots standing on the floor, and quickly he put them on.

Then he waded to the fireplace to take the saucepan off the stove; but, dear me, the soup was now so deep that when he got near the fire it had risen higher than the tops of his boots, and soaked down into them.

'Ooh! It's burning me!' yelled Chinky, and he ran out into his garden. But the soup followed him there, and soon the garden path was a stream of onion soup.

Then Chinky burst into tears and ran into Mother Tiptap's, weeping bitterly.

'Quick! Quick!' he cried. 'Come and make the soup stop, Mother Tiptap!'

Mother Tiptap ran out, and when she saw the soup pouring out of the cottage she knew what had happened.

'You shouldn't have listened underneath my window this morning,' she said. 'This just serves you right, Chinky. *I* don't know how to stop the spell. Dame Twinkle was just going to tell me when she heard you sneeze, and after that she wouldn't say another word about it, in case you were listening again. If you want to make the soup stop coming out of your saucepan, you'd better go and ask her what to do.'

'I daren't go to Dame Twinkle!' wailed Chinky. 'She

would spank me hard, I know.'

'She certainly would,' said Mother Tiptap. 'But what else can you do?'

'I'll just get my bag and go straight off to my brother, who lives at the other end of Fairyland,' said Chinky, wiping his eyes. 'I shall never come back *here* again, I can tell you that! How could I live in my house, now it's all over soup, I should like to know! You're welcome to Primrose Cottage, if you like to clear the mess.'

With that Chinky went to a window, put in his hand, and lifted his bag from a chair. Then off he went to catch the six o'clock bus, and that was the last that Mother Tiptap ever heard of him.

She sent a message to Dame Twinkle, who came along at once. How she laughed when she heard what had happened!

'It serves the prying little creature right!' she said. '*He'll* never come back to bother you again, old friend.'

'The soup is still pouring out of the saucepan,' said Mother Tiptap. 'How do you stop it?'

'I was just going to tell you when I heard that horrid little Chinky sneezing,' said Dame Twinkle. 'Look!'

She clapped her hands seven times, and called out loudly: 'Carrot, enough! Come to me!'

At once the carrot in the saucepan flew out, and came straight to Dame Twinkle's hand. The soup immediately stopped pouring from the pan, and in half a moment all the soup in the garden and cottage dried up by magic! Only half a saucepanful remained, sizzling away on the stove.

'Chinky ought to have clapped his hands and called

out "Carrot, enough! Come to me!" as soon as the pan was full of soup,' said Dame Twinkle. 'But, of course, he didn't know that.'

'Well, he'll never come back here again,' said Mother Tiptap, pleased, 'and he said I was welcome to his cottage, if I liked to have it. Do come and live there, Dame Twinkle. You are always saying that your house is too cold for you.'

'Well, I will,' said Dame Twinkle, and the very next day she moved in. All Chinky's dirty, broken old furniture was burnt, and his ragged curtains were pulled down and used for floor-cloths. Mother Tiptap was delighted to see pretty blue curtains hanging at the windows, and to hear Dame Twinkle singing happily away next door.

The garden soon began to look trim and neat, and the two friends often helped one another in their weeding. And after a good day's work, they went to supper with one another, and made soup with Mister Chippy's spell.

Sometimes they say, 'Do you remember when Chinky tried to make the soup, and it wouldn't stop?'

And then Dame Twinkle and Mother Tiptap laugh till the tears run down their cheeks!

Jimmy was staying with his Auntie Susan and Uncle Jack. His mother and daddy were away, and were not coming back for three weeks.

Jimmy liked to stay with his aunt and uncle. They had a lovely farm, with pigs, cows, horses, hens, geese, ducks, and goats. There was always something to do and see, and Jimmy was very happy.

But there was something that rather worried him – and that was his birthday. It came on September the third, and Jimmy's mother always made it a perfectly lovely day for him. He had a cake with candles on, he had lots of fine presents, and his mother always let him choose a treat. Sometimes Jimmy chose a party, once he had asked to go to the Zoo, and the last time he had had a fine picnic.

What worried him was that Auntie Susan might forget his birthday. He knew that in the cupboard upstairs were two large parcels that Daddy and Mummy had let him take with him, to be opened on his birthday, But Auntie Susan had the key to the cupboard, and Jimmy thought that if she forgot his birthday, he really *couldn't* ask her to let him get the parcels.

'Mummy says people never talk about their own birthday, or ask about it,' said Jimmy to himself. 'And I promised her I wouldn't keep reminding Auntie Susan about it. But I shall be perfectly *miserable* if she forgets. A birthday only comes once a year, and I couldn't bear to miss mine.'

It was one of Jimmy's duties to tear off the days of the calendar that hung on the wall by his uncle's desk. Day by day his birthday came nearer, and still his aunt said nothing about it. Then one day when he tore off the day from the calendar he saw that his birthday was the very next day.

'I do wonder if Auntie Susan will remember it,' he said to himself. 'I would so love to have the presents that Mummy and Daddy got for me, but I don't see how I can ask for them, because if I do Auntie will think I am reminding her that it's my birthday. Well, if she forgets, I must just put up with it, that's all.'

The next day the calendar said September the third, Jimmy's birthday. Jimmy looked at it sadly, as he tore off September the second. Nobody had wished him many happy returns of the day, no cards had come for him, and no presents. There wasn't even a card from Mummy and Daddy.

'Everyone's forgotten me,' he thought. 'Old Cook at home, who always made me a lovely cake, has forgotten too. What a perfectly horrid birthday!'

When the postman came again in the middle of the morning, Jimmy ran to meet him, hoping that there might be a birthday card from his mother. But there were only three letters for Uncle Jack – nothing else at all. It was dreadfully disappointing.

'Perhaps there'll be a special cake for me at tea-time,'

thought Jimmy. But there wasn't. There wasn't any cake at all!

'Only bread and butter!' thought Jimmy, as he looked at the table. 'Goodness, what a horrid birthday! How I wish I was at home with Mummy and Daddy! And, oh, how I do wish I could have their presents out of the cupboard upstairs! I really think I shall have to ask for them at the end of the day. I'll ask if I can stay up for an extra half hour, as it's my birthday, and then I'll unpack the two presents.'

But what a shock for Jimmy! When six o'clock came, half an hour *before* his bedtime, Auntie Susan came into the room where he was playing.

'I want you to go to bed half an hour earlier tonight, Jimmy,' she said. 'Tomorrow will be rather a special day, and I want to pack you off early tonight.'

Well, if that wasn't dreadful! A special day indeed! Perhaps Uncle Jack was going to sell his pigs at the market, or Auntie Susan was going to bake the bread – and they called that a special day, when today had been his birthday, and nobody had taken any notice of it!

Poor Jimmy! He really felt as if he was going to cry, and because he was a big boy he didn't like to let his aunt see the tears in his eyes. So he quickly kissed her, and ran straight out of the room upstairs to bed.

When he was in bed, with the sunshine still streaming in through the window, he couldn't stop the tears running down his cheeks. It had been such a very dreadful birthday. Suddenly before he could wipe the tears away, the door opened, and his aunt came in.

'What! In bed already!' she cried. 'What a good boy

you are, Jimmy! But what's the matter, dear? Surely you're not crying! What are you worrying about?'

'N-n-n-nothing,' said Jimmy.

'Oh, yes, you are,' said his aunt, sitting down on his bed. 'Tell me, or I shall be very sad.'

'It's only about my birthday,' said Jimmy at last. 'Everybody's forgotten it, and it made me unhappy. I didn't like to ask you for the two presents from Mummy and Daddy in the cupboard on the landing.'

'But what do you mean, dear?' asked his aunt, in astonishment. 'You haven't had your birthday yet?'

'Yes, it was today,' said Jimmy. 'September the third is my birthday, Auntie Susan. Perhaps you didn't know.'

'Of course I knew!' said his aunt. 'But today is September the *second*, Jimmy. *Tomorrow* is your birthday! Don't you remember that I told you tomorrow was a special day? Well, you silly boy, it was your birthday I meant!'

'But, Auntie, the calendar downstairs that I pull off every day, says September the third *today*,' said Jimmy. 'Really it does.'

'Well, let's come and see,' said his aunt. So Jimmy got out of bed, and together they went downstairs to the room where the calendar hung. Uncle Jack was sitting there, and he *was* surprised to see them.

'Hallo! Hallo!' he said. 'What's all this? I thought Jimmy was in bed.'

'So he was,' said Aunt Susan. 'And what do you think, Jack – poor Jimmy thought that today was his birthday, not tomorrow. He said the calendar here said it was today.'

Sure enough, the calendar *did* say September the third!

'Oh!' said Uncle Jack, with a laugh. 'I meant to have spoken to Jimmy about that calendar. One day, about a week ago, I forgot that Jimmy was tearing off the days for me, and *I* tore off one as well! So it made the calendar a day wrong – it was always saying the date for tomorrow instead of for today. But I quite forgot to tell him, so he didn't know.'

'Goodness me!' said Jimmy. 'So it isn't September the third after all – it's only the second. And today wasn't my birthday – it's tomorrow!'

'Of course it is,' said his aunt, hugging him. 'I thought you'd forgotten all about it, because you didn't say a word, and I thought it would be a lovely surprise for you to wake up tomorrow and suddenly find it was a birthday, so *I* didn't say anything either!'

'Hurrah!' said Jimmy, skipping round the room. 'It's my birthday tomorrow. I shall have a proper one after all!'

'Of course you will,' said his aunt and uncle together. Then they bundled him off to bed and told him to go to sleep.

And what a birthday he had next day! The postman brought him fifteen cards and seven parcels. His father's and mother's presents were on the table, and there was a big parcel from Auntie Susan too.

'My present's out in the yard,' said Uncle Jack. 'Auntie wouldn't let me bring it in at breakfast-time!'

Jimmy ran out to see what it was – and guess! It was a little black and white puppy. Jimmy was full of delight.

It was just what he had longed for.

In his mother's parcel was a fine fort for soldiers, and in his father's parcel was a toy aeroplane. So you can guess what an exciting time he had! His aunt gave him a set of garden tools, and besides those he had books, chocolates, games, and a clockwork engine.

'Now what about a birthday treat?' asked Uncle Jack, when they had all finished breakfast. 'What would you like to do?'

'Go to market with you, Uncle,' said Jimmy, at once. This was what he had always longed to do, but had never liked to ask for before.

'Come along then!' said his uncle. 'We must soon start.'

'Be home in good time for tea!' called his aunt, as they set off. 'There's a birthday cake!'

What a lovely day that was! What a lot of pigs and cows, horses, hens and ducks Jimmy saw! And what fun to climb into uncle's cart and jog home to tea, knowing there was a birthday cake waiting for him.

It really was a beautiful cake. It had Jimmy's name on in pink, and 'A Happy Birthday' in blue. It had eight candles on, one for each of Jimmy's years, and Jimmy lighted them himself. There were two kinds of jam, some new honey, some chocolate buns and jelly and cream. So you can guess it was a really proper birthday tea.

Jimmy stayed up till half-past seven, for a treat, and when he went to bed he was so tired and happy that he really couldn't keep his eyes open. Auntie Susan tucked him into bed and kissed him good night.

'It's been the nicest birthday I've ever had!' said

Jimmy. 'What a silly I was to think it had been forgotten!'

And off he went to sleep, and dreamt that he was
flying off to market in his new toy aeroplane!

17. Pickles and the Magic Chop

Pickles was a little black dog. He belonged to old Mother Nod, and he was a dreadful little rascal. Mother Nod was not rich, so she couldn't afford to give Pickles much meat, but she bought him plenty of fine, dry biscuits, and gave him a plateful every day.

One day Pickles passed the shop of Mr. Mutton the butcher, and he smelt the meat there. Ooh! What a lovely smell! Pickles thought it was the nicest shop in the village. Mr. Mutton was at the back of the shop carving up a joint, and there was no one in the street at all.

Just by Pickles's nose hung a string of sausages. Pickles snatched at them, and then galloped off in a hurry, dragging the sausages behind him.

And what a feast he had in the back yard when he got home. Mother Nod couldn't think why he wouldn't eat any biscuits at his dinner-time, but Pickles didn't tell her that he had had a whole string of sausages. He knew she would be very cross indeed to hear that.

Now Mr. Mutton was angry to find his nice sausages gone, and he kept a sharp look-out for the thief, thinking that whoever had stolen them would be sure to come along again and try to steal something else.

But Pickles was too sharp for that. He knew Mr. Mutton would be looking out for him, so he didn't go near the butcher's shop at all. Instead he went to Mr.

Haddock the fishmonger. The fish didn't smell quite so good as the sausages, but Pickles was hungry, and he really didn't mind what he had for his dinner.

Mr. Haddock was adding up the bills in his little counting-house, and there was no one else near his shop at all. Pickles put his two front paws on the marble slab where the fish were, and snapped at three fine bloaters. Then off he ran with them, helter-skelter down the road, and didn't once stop till he was safe in Mother Nod's back yard.

What a lovely dinner he had! And what a shock poor Mr. Haddock got when he found his three best bloaters gone.

'*I'll* watch out for that thief!' he said. 'Whoever it is, I'll catch him next time.'

But Pickles was much too artful to go near Mr. Haddock's shop again. He went to old Dame Crinkle's kitchen door and peeped in. He had smelt such a fine smell that he felt sure there was something to be found there.

And so there was! For Dame Crinkle had just baked a meat pie, and taken it out of the oven. She had put it on the window-sill to cool, and then she had gone into her parlour to water the plants there.

In a trice Pickles slipped into the kitchen, put his paws on the window-sill, and picked up the pie in his mouth. The dish was still hot and burnt the naughty dog's mouth, but he didn't mind that. Off he went, carrying the pie carefully, and what a feast he had when he got safely to Mother Nod's house without anyone seeing him.

When poor Dame Crinkle found that her lovely meat pie was gone, she was in a terrible way. But she couldn't even *guess* who the thief was.

Pickles stole a great many more things. There was a currant cake he took from Mother Buttercup's, a pile of sausage rolls from Mr. Binny's, a whole joint of meat from Tippy's house, and a large ham from Mrs. Wait-abit's.

Soon everyone in the village was puzzled and angry. They thought that it must be a tramp who was wandering about stealing things, but the funny thing was that nobody had even *seen* the tramp.

'Well, we must lay a trap for the thief, whoever he is,' said Mr. Binny. 'All next week we must none of us leave a single thing about that the thief can take. Lock up everything in your larders. Tell Mr. Mutton and Mr. Haddock to close down the glass windows over the front of their shops, and to keep a boy on the look-out. And then we'll lay a trap!'

'What sort of trap?' asked all the people.

'Wait and see!' said Mr. Binny, and he put on his hat and walked up the hill to where the wise woman lived. There he bought something from her, and came back with it wrapped carefully in his best silk handkerchief.

Then he bought a fine meaty chop from Mr. Mutton, and took it home. After that he unwrapped his silk handkerchief, and everyone peeped to see what he had inside it.

'It's a spell,' said Mr. Binny. 'It's so small you can hardly see it. I'm going to put it into a little hole in this meat – and then we shall see what happens when the thief comes along and takes this fine chop!'

He stuffed the spell into a hole in the chop, and then he put the meat on an enamel dish. He put the dish out on his window-sill, shut the window, and sent everyone away and waited.

Very soon Pickles came along, sniffing here and there to see what he could find to eat that morning. He went all round the village, but everyone had done as Mr. Binny said, and had carefully put all their food away in the larder. There was nothing for Pickles at all. He was dreadfully disappointed.

But wait a minute! What was this he smelt at Mr. Binny's? Surely it was nice fresh meat! Where was it?

Pickles smelt all round, and at last found the chop on the dish outside the window. In a trice he leapt up, snatched the chop from the dish and tore off with it to Mother Nod's back yard. When he got there he put the chop down and sniffed at it. He could smell the spell in it, and he wondered what it was; but, oh, dear me, as soon as his nose sniffed at that chop a very strange thing happened!

It gave a squeak, and jumped right on to the top of Pickles's nose! There it stuck fast, and no matter what Pickles did he couldn't shake it off. It held tightly there, and, oh, what a funny sight he looked, with a large chop standing neatly on his nose.

Pickles tried to scrape it off with first one paw and then another, but he couldn't move it. It stuck there by magic, and the frightened dog soon knew that he would have to leave it there. He crept into his kennel and lay down miserably, wondering what he should do. He was very hungry, and the smell of the chop made him hungrier still, but he couldn't get at it, no matter how he tried.

Soon Mother Nod came and called him to go to his plate of biscuits, but he didn't stir. He was too much ashamed of showing Mother Nod what he had on his nose. Presently she came to find him, and when she saw that he was in his kennel she took him by the collar and pulled him out.

'What are you doing, Pickles?' she asked. 'Didn't you hear? Good gracious me! Whatever's this? What *have* you got on your nose?'

She *was* astonished to see the chop there! She couldn't understand it at all. She tried to pull it off, but it hurt Pickles, and when he howled in pain she stopped.

'However did it come there?' she asked. 'Well, this is really a most extraordinary thing! I must take you to Mr. Mutton the butcher and see if *he* can get it off for you!'

So poor Pickles was put on the lead and taken all through the village to Mr. Mutton's, and as soon as the butcher saw the naughty little dog he knew who the thief was! He pointed his finger at Pickles, and began to laugh, for really it was a funny sight to see a chop sitting on the dog's nose.

'So *you're* the thief!' he said, when he had stopped laughing. 'Well, I've no pity for you. You'll just have to be laughed at till the spell wears away. That will teach you not to steal.'

Mother Nod was very much upset when she heard what had happened. She asked Mr. Mutton to whip

Pickles hard, and the butcher was glad to do so, for he had not forgotten the sausages that were stolen. Then Pickles was taken home, and how everyone laughed at him!

But that wasn't the worst. In the night all the cats round about smelt the chop, and came to see where it was. They crowded into Pickles's kennel, and tried to snatch it off his nose. Pickles barked and snapped at them, but they wouldn't leave him alone. At last, when they found that they really couldn't get the chop away from him, they went back to their homes – but poor Pickles's nose *was* scratched.

Next day it was the dogs who came sniffing round his kennel. When they saw the chop on Pickles's nose they were full of surprise.

'He's doing a trick,' they said. 'How silly of him, when he might eat the chop. Let's get it!'

So they all rushed at his kennel, and soon there was a dreadful fight going on, and it wasn't until Mother Nod came out with a stick that the dogs went away.

Poor Pickles was bruised and bitten. How he did wish he had never stolen anything! What a dreadful thing it was to be a thief! He would never, never, in all his life take anything that didn't belong to him.

As Pickles lay sadly in his kennel, thinking these thoughts, the spell began to wear away. As long as he was not sorry for what he had done the spell stayed fast in the chop; but as soon as the naughty little dog began to feel ashamed and sad, the spell loosened.

And one morning Pickles woke up with the chop off his nose, lying on the floor beside him! How joyful he was! He picked it up in his mouth and trotted into Mother Nod's kitchen with it. He laid it down at her feet.

'Wuff!' he said. 'Wuff-wuff, wuffy-wuff! Wuff!'

Mother Nod knew perfectly well what he was saying. He meant, 'Look! I'm sorry, very sorry! Forgive me!'

'I'll forgive you,' she said. 'But I think you ought to go round to all the people you stole from, Pickles, and say you're sorry to them too.'

So the little dog went round to everyone, and wuffed hard. And they all forgave him and patted him on the head. Mr. Binny took the magic chop and threw it into his fire, where it sizzled away merrily in tongues of green flame.

'Well, the spell did its work!' he said. 'Ha ha! How funny you looked, Pickles! Now mind you never steal again!'

'Wuff!' said Pickles, and off he ran home as fast as he could. And never did he take anything again that didn't belong to him, but was an honest, faithful little dog for the rest of his life.

'Mummy!' cried Ann, dancing into the kitchen, where her mother was making cakes. 'I've got an invitation to Doreen's party. May I go?'

'If you're a good girl,' said her mother. 'You can wear your new blue dress.'

'But what about shoes?' asked Ann. 'I haven't any blue ones to match, Mummy. And my old party ones are no use now because they don't fit me.'

'Well, perhaps I'll buy you a new pair of blue ones,' said her mother. 'But you must just show me how good you can be, Ann, or I certainly shan't buy you any.'

Ann made up her mind to be as good as gold. But somehow or other things seemed to go wrong. Ann dropped one of her mother's very best cups and broke it. Then she dropped a bowl of flowers she was carrying, and that broke too, and all the water went on to the carpet.

Ann's mother was vexed.

'You're a careless little girl,' she said.

Ann said she was sorry. She did hope her mother wouldn't be cross enough not to buy the blue shoes. She determined to be very careful indeed for the few days before the party.

Soon another unlucky thing happened. Ann lost her new gloves! Then her mother really *was* cross!

'You'll have just one more chance!' she said to the little girl. 'If you do one more careless or naughty thing you shall not have your new shoes!'

Ann knew that her mother meant what she said, and she began to be really afraid she wouldn't be able to go to the party. So for the next two days she was a very good little girl indeed.

Then came the day before the party.

'Mummy, may I go and buy those new blue shoes with you?' asked Ann.

'Yes,' said her mother. 'I'll take you this afternoon. But this morning I want you to take a message for me to Mrs. Robinson. Here is the note. Now go straight there and back. You just have got time before dinner, so don't dawdle as you did last time. If you do, dinner will be cold, and we shall probably miss the only bus into the town to get your shoes.'

'All right, Mummy!' said Ann, joyfully. 'I'll be sure to be back in time!'

Off she ran with the note. She went down the lane, and over the stile into the fields. Soon she came to the wood, and took the path that ran through it. She didn't stop for anything, not even when she saw some lovely foxgloves blooming all together.

In an hour's time she came to Mrs. Robinson's. She left the note, took the answer, and turned to go home again.

'I shall be home before Mummy expects me!' she thought.

Now, as she went back through the wood, she chanced to hear a cry. It was a funny sort of sound, not like a bird or animal. Ann wondered what it could be. She stopped a moment, and looked through the trees to where she thought the cry had come from. And as she stopped someone came running out from the trees towards her.

Ann stared in surprise – for it was an elf! He was very small, tinier than Ann, and he was crying.

'Little girl, little girl,' he cried, 'come and help me! My butterflies are all entangled in the thorns!'

Ann ran through the trees to where he pointed. There she saw an astonishing sight. There was a beautiful little carriage, drawn by five blue butterflies, but somehow or other they had got themselves caught in a bramble bush, and their pretty wings were being torn as they struggled to free themselves.

'Could you help me?' asked the elf, drying his eyes. 'If you could hold the reins tightly I think I could get their wings free. But it will take rather a long time.'

'Oh, dear!' said Ann, in dismay. 'I'd love to help you, little elf, but my mother says I *must* get home quickly. You see, she's going to take me into town to buy me a pair of blue shoes for tomorrow's party, and if I'm late she won't take me, and anyhow we should miss the bus. I'm afraid I can't stop to help you.'

'All right,' said the elf, tears streaming down his face again. 'I quite understand. But, oh, my poor butterflies! They'll be torn to bits. If you meet another little girl who hasn't got to buy shoes for the party would you tell her to come and help me?'

Ann looked at him, and then looked at the butterflies. She knew quite well that she wouldn't meet anyone else going through the woods. She didn't know *what* to do.

Then she suddenly made up her mind.

'Don't cry,' she said. 'I'll stay and help. Perhaps I'll be in time for dinner after all.'

'Oh, thank you a thousand times!' cried the elf, wiping his eyes. 'Come on, then. Hold the reins, and I'll go and calm the butterflies.'

Ann climbed into the little carriage, and held the reins firmly. The elf ran to his butterflies and began to disentangle their wings from the cruel thorns. One by one he freed them. It took a very long time, for he was so afraid of tearing their beautiful wings. But at last it was done.

'There!' he said, joyfully. 'They're all free now. Thank you so much, little girl. I do hope you'll be in time.'

'I hope so too,' said Ann. 'Well, good-bye and I hope you get home safely.'

She ran off. She knew it must be very late. She ran faster than she had ever run before. She panted and puffed, and didn't stop once till she reached home and ran up the garden path.

'*Well!*' said her mother. 'What in the world have you been doing to be so late? Dinner is over long ago and the bus is just starting.'

'Oh, Mummy!' said Ann, nearly crying. 'I really couldn't help it. You see, I met an elf and—'

'Nonsense!' said her mother, crossly. 'You've just been dawdling again. Well, you can't have your blue shoes, that's all.'

'But, Mummy, I can't go to the party unless I have them!' said Ann. 'I haven't any others I can wear.'

'Well, it's your own fault!' said her mother. 'You're a silly little girl. Now go and eat your dinner, and don't let me hear a word more.'

Poor Ann! She went and sat down at the table, but she couldn't eat anything. She was so dreadfully disappointed. She saw the bus go off, and a big lump came into her throat. No shoes and no party! She was very sad.

She had to look after the baby all the afternoon, and after tea she had her sewing to do. She went early to bed, for she wanted to go to sleep and forget her disappointment.

At six o'clock the next morning she got up to light the fire and get her mother a cup of tea, for she was a very useful little girl. She opened the front door to air the cottage – and then she stopped and stared in surprise.

On the doorstep was a box. It was bright yellow, and was tied with blue ribbon. A little label hung from it that said: 'For the little girl who helped my butterflies.'

Ann picked up the box. She quickly took off the ribbon and opened the lid. And, oh, my! what *do* you think was inside? Why, the prettiest, daintiest pair of blue satin shoes you could possibly imagine, and instead of buckles they had two tiny blue butterflies, just like the big ones she had helped the day before.

Ann cried out with joy. She sat down on the doorstep and tried the shoes on. They fitted her exactly – and didn't they look lovely! They were the prettiest pair she had ever seen in her life, far, far nicer than any she could have bought in a shop.

She ran upstairs to her mother.

'Mummy, Mummy!' she cried. 'Look, the elf has brought me some shoes for the party! I expect he knew that I couldn't go and buy any because he made me late!'

Then, of course, her mother had to hear all the story, and she was very glad when she knew what had happened.

'Well, you deserve them,' she said to Ann. 'I really didn't believe you had met an elf, but I do now, for these shoes are fairy ones, if ever shoes were! You will look lovely in them!'

'Hurrah!' said Ann. 'Everything has come right now! I *shall* enjoy the party!' And she did!

Enid Blyton for Younger Readers

You have just finished reading an Enid
Blyton book which we hope you enjoyed.
Have you read the following delightful Enid
books published by Dragon for your
pleasure?

EIGHT O'CLOCK TALES   17½p
THE RED STORY BOOK   17½p
THE BLUE STORY BOOK   17½p
THE YELLOW STORY BOOK   17½p
THE GREEN STORY BOOK   17½p
TEN-MINUTE TALES   17½p
THE LAND OF FAR-BEYOND   17½p
THE BOOK OF NAUGHTY CHILDREN
17½p
TALES OF BETSY MAY   17½p
BILLY BOB TALES   17½p
THE CHILDREN'S LIFE OF CHRIST
17½p
TALES FROM THE BIBLE   17½p
THE SECOND BOOK OF
NAUGHTY CHILDREN   20p
FIFTEEN-MINUTE TALES   20p

Available from booksellers everywhere.
If your nearest bookseller doesn't have the
book you want write to us at this address:

The Editor, Dragon Books, 3 Upper James
Street, London, W1R 4BP

The Winter of Enchantment

Victoria Walker   20p

A magic mirror enables Sebastian to travel
from his Victorian world of winter snow and
Mrs Parkin to a magic world of Melissa,
Mantari, a wicked Enchanter and many
other exciting people. Melissa, who is a very
pretty girl, has been imprisoned in a large
house by the wicked Enchanter who intends
keeping her there for ever and ever.
Sebastian first meets Melissa through the
magic mirror and resolves to do everything
in his power to free her. This involves
collecting together all the wicked
Enchanter's 'Power Objects': the mirror, a
teapot, a silver fish, an emerald and a green
rose, throwing them into a magic well and so
destroying the Enchanter's power.

This wonderful book follows in the great
tradition of E. Nesbit magic books, and a
very worthy successor it is. It will appeal to
both boys and girls in a very wide age group.

Illustrated by the author

Look Books

An exciting and colourful collection of non-fiction paperbacks for children.

LOOK AT THEATRES
LOOK AT CHURCHES
LOOK AT CASTLES
LOOK AT ZOOS
LOOK AT CARS
LOOK AT ROMANS
LOOK AT AIRCRAFT
LOOK AT STARS
LOOK AT PONIES
LOOK AT BRITISH WILD ANIMALS
LOOK AT PARLIAMENT
LOOK AT RAILWAYS
LOOK AT THE CIRCUS
LOOK AT HOUSES
LOOK AT BIRDS
LOOK AT AFRICAN WILD LIFE
LOOK AT DOGS
LOOK AT SUBMARINES
LOOK AT LIGHTHOUSES

Only 20p each – packed with useful information, written by well-known authors, and illustrated.
Ask your bookseller to show you them.